SHATTERED

TRIPLE CANOPY
BOOK 7

RILEY EDWARDS

BE A REBEL

SHATTERED
Triple Canopy 7

This is a work of fiction. Names, characters, businesses, places, events, and incidents are either the products of the author's imagination or used in a fictitious manner. Any resemblance to actual persons, living or dead, or actual events is purely coincidental.

Copyright © 2022 by Riley Edwards

All rights reserved. This book or any portion thereof may not be reproduced or used in any manner whatsoever without the express written permission of the publisher except for the use of brief quotations in a book review.

Cover design: Lori Jackson Designs

Written by: Riley Edwards

Published by: Riley Edwards/Rebels Romance

Edited by: Rebecca Hodgkins

Proofreader: Julie Deaton, Kendall Barnett

Book Name: Shattered

Paperback ISBN: 978-1951567316

First edition: October 27, 2022

Copyright © 2022 Riley Edwards

All rights reserved

To my family - my team – my tribe.
This is for you.

CONTENTS

Prologue	1
Chapter 1	5
Chapter 2	18
Chapter 3	26
Chapter 4	45
Chapter 5	57
Chapter 6	73
Chapter 7	85
Chapter 8	92
Chapter 9	111
Chapter 10	127
Chapter 11	136
Chapter 12	143
Chapter 13	162
Chapter 14	174
Chapter 15	185
Chapter 16	199
Chapter 17	207
Also by Riley Edwards	211
Audio	215
Be A Rebel	217

PROLOGUE

I had to have the wrong address.

I looked down at the slip of paper in my hand and then back at the apartment complex.

It wasn't the worst I'd ever seen but it did not look like a place a man called Phoenix Kent would live. A man who looked like Phoenix, who was that tall and devastatingly hot and was a real-life hero needed to live in a Bruce Wayne-style lair. Not a crappy apartment complex.

I was undecided about what to say when I saw him. *Thank you for saving my son's life* didn't seem like enough, but at the same time, it said it all.

Phoenix had saved Griff.

And that night, I had been such a wreck I hadn't been able to tell him thank you. And too many weeks had passed since I'd last seen him. And it would be many months before the Hope Center would be repaired after the fire. And when it was, I was uncertain if I could send Griff back there.

So the time was nigh.

I climbed the stairs and looked for apartment 330.

It was now or never.

I raised my hand, sucked in a breath, and knocked.

I waited but no one answered. Maybe he was at work. I was digging through my purse to find a scrap of paper to write him a note when the door opened.

My eyes lifted and I sucked in a breath.

Sweet baby Jesus.

I had to blink to make sure I wasn't seeing things.

Nope. Still shirtless.

The last time I'd seen Phoenix he'd been soaking wet and covered in soot, carrying my son out of a burning building. At the time, all I could think about was my boy. Days later when I calmed down, I had to admit my mind had lapsed into inappropriate thoughts.

Because seeing Phoenix running, soaking wet, covered in soot, carrying my boy out of a burning building was the sexiest thing I'd ever witnessed in my whole sorry life.

So, it was safe to say I'd never clapped eyes on a man as hot as Phoenix Kent.

But shirtless, with his broad chest on display, not to mention the tattoo covering his left pec, shoulder, and arm, plus the well-defined ridges on his abdomen?

Good Lawd, the man was a sex God.

A sex God I wanted to...

"Wren?"

"Yeah. Um. Phoenix."

Christ almighty, get a grip.

"Yeah, sorry to bother you. I wanted to talk to you."

Well, no shit, Sherlock, you're at his house. Why else would you be there if not to talk?

Climb on top of him and ride him.

He roughly dragged his hand through his hair.

"Now's not a good time."

Holy shit, was there someone in there with him?

Did he have a girlfriend?

Of course he did. A man as hot as Phoenix would definitely have a girlfriend or ten.

Shit, I was so dumb.

"Right. Sorry."

I turned to leave but his hand shot out and wrapped around my wrist. The zap of awareness was so strong it took me by surprise. When I looked back at Phoenix, his eyes were aimed down where his big hand circled my wrist. I was not a small woman—at five-ten, not a lot of men could make me feel small. But Phoenix did. My wrist looked almost dainty in his grip when it most certainly was not.

"Wait. Let me get dressed. We can go somewhere and talk."

"No, it's okay. I shouldn't've come by."

"Just wait here a second while I get dressed," he insisted.

"Um. Sure."

"Okay. Good. One second."

He dropped my hand, closed the door, and I hightailed my ass down the stairs. I didn't stop running until I got into my car. Then I sped away like a coward.

A smart coward.

A coward who could not afford to fall in love. And I would. Phoenix Kent was a man a woman would fall for. She'd get lost in those blue eyes and all that taut skin. But mostly she'd fall in love because he was a real-life hero.

I would write him a letter. Tell him thank you, then I'd never contact him again and do my best to forget him.

But he'd saved my son's life so I knew that would be an impossibility.

What I didn't know as I sped away was that Phoenix Kent didn't feel like forgetting me.

1

Have you ever had your life flash before your eyes? No, not your life, a moment in time. A conversation, an incident, a trauma, a *moment* that played and replayed over and over in your mind. All of the things you said or didn't say or wish you would've said. Things you wished you would've done or regretted what you *had* done. Moments when you wished you were brave—be it brave enough to walk away or brave enough to stay or brave enough to stand up for yourself.

I had so many of those moments that if I wasn't careful —really careful—these thoughts consumed me.

I was a half-woman pretending to be whole. A single mother who had no other choice but to pretend. I had a boy to raise and it was my job to see to it he turned out to be a good man. The kind of man who would be strong and loving, who would be gentle and kind, care about those around him, be loyal, be brave, and tell the truth. A man who would be everything his father and my father were not. There was no other choice—Griffin needed to be those things. Not only because it was my responsibility to turn out a good citizen and send a decent man into the world, but *I* needed to do those things because I had something to prove. To myself and to Griffin. Not all men were cheaters and liars and criminals. Men—real men—were protectors, both emotionally and physically.

Real men loved openly. They didn't steal and rob and murder. They didn't break promises. They shielded those they loved from harm, and they most especially weren't the cause of hurt and heartbreak.

I had to believe nurture could and would overcome nature. I had to believe that whatever sickness my father had in him hadn't infested me. I had to believe that whatever drove my ex-husband to do the things he did wouldn't live in my son.

But I was failing.

Miserably.

These were my thoughts as I watched Griff mowing the backyard. This was my curse—overthinking. The cross I was left to bear because no one in my life ever thought—not about the consequences of their actions, not the pain of their betrayal, not the broken promises, not the day-to-day tasks of life, not the trail of destruction they left behind. No one ever gave a thought to those things, which meant my brain never shut down.

So I was deep in my misery, thinking about all the moments in my life I'd screwed up. All the wrong turns. All the ways I was failing at this parenting gig when there was a knock on my front door.

We'd been in Georgia for three months and in those three months, I had made zero effort to make friends. Sure, I was friendly with my neighbors and coworkers but the niceties we shared couldn't be interpreted as friendships. With school back in session Griff was picking up a few buds here and there, but I doubted teenage boys came knocking at ten o'clock on a Saturday morning. Hell, I had to drag my son's rear end out of bed under the threat of throwing his Xbox in the trash if he didn't get his butt in gear and get his chores done. In other words, I was not expecting company.

Therefore, I was wholly and completely unprepared to open my door and find Phoenix Kent on my front porch scowling at me. Not that a woman could prepare for the man's extreme masculine beauty.

I felt my chest compress along with a multitude of emotions as they rushed over me—fear, anticipation, dread, embarrassment, and lust all blended together in a complex mixture of panic. Overwhelming panic. Run-for-the-hills, slam-the-door-in-his-face panic.

"You're alive." That was Phoenix's strange opening. He said those words while his icy blue eyes narrowed, blasting me with ominous waves of pissed-off-ness.

And since he was for some unknown reason angry, I reciprocated in kind. Albeit unwisely since Phoenix did pissed-off way better than me.

"Indeed. Is there a reason I wouldn't be?"

Those aforementioned blue eyes turned icier and he bit out, "Called you five times and texted you seven."

Yup, that was the truth. The first call came in less than three minutes after I'd sped away from his apartment building in a haze of humiliation. Part of that embarrassment stemmed from lusting after a man who I had no business lusting after.

But the real reason I'd fled and then ignored his calls for a week was that when I looked at Phoenix, I saw myself.

It was like we were kindred spirits. He lived his life behind a wall the same as I did. Undoubtedly our bricks were carved from different circumstances but the cement holding those blocks in place was the same—pain. I had no idea what had caused his or how many layers deep it ran, but I knew pain when I saw it. And I also knew from the moment I saw him I wanted to know what had caused it. I wanted to dig it out, and for the first time in ten years since mine had layered on so thickly that I could hardly breathe, I wanted to delegate the monumental task of excavating myself out from behind my wall to him.

I fled because I wanted to see to his pain. I wanted to know what could make a man as big and strong as Phoenix Kent hide. I fled because I knew it wouldn't take much for me to fall in love with him. I ran to my car as fast as my feet would carry me because I knew Phoenix—a man who could have any woman he wanted with nothing more than a smile—would never want a middle-aged divorcée with a teenage son. But there was knowing and then there was *knowing*.

Therefore, I did the smart thing for once in my life and got gone as quickly as I could.

"We need to talk," he continued.

My earlier panic intensified. I didn't want to talk to Phoenix; so far, my plan to avoid him was working. Not that it wouldn't, the only place I'd ever seen him was when he volunteered at the Hope Center, and since the...

Nope.

I viciously shoved those thoughts away and clutched the door. Watching my son almost die was one of those moments that ravaged my soul. I couldn't think about it without starting to hyperventilate.

"Listen, I'm sorry I showed up at your house unannounced. That was uncool."

"You already apologized."

"Okay. Then I'm sorry I interrupted—"

"Interrupted?"

I really, seriously did not want to get into this with him. Especially with Griffin close to being done with the lawn.

Since I didn't want to talk about that day or how embarrassed I was when he denied me entry to his home, I remained silent.

"What exactly did you think you were interrupting, Wren?"

I'd never been particularly fond of my name but, Lawd Almighty I loved the way he said it.

No way was I going to tell him what I thought I'd interrupted. There was no chance in hell I wanted to talk about why he answered the door looking like he'd just rolled out of bed and only had time to pull on a pair of jeans. No way was I going to think about why the top button on those jeans was undone. And I really wasn't going to allow myself to think about the woman who he'd left in his bed.

And since I did not lie, not ever, not even when I knew the other person didn't want to hear the truth—though I was nice about it—I did what I always did. I changed the subject.

"I should've called. I wanted to thank you for what you did. For saving Griff. And also, I wanted to tell you I was glad you were okay."

He completely ignored me and swerved the conversation back around.

"Let's go back to what you thought you were interrupting."

No way.

Not a chance in hell.

"I should've texted you back. That was rude."

I wished I was the lying type so I could make up a story about how I got busy and forgot to answer. But the truth was I'd read each of his seven texts several times over the last few days and each time I read them I tapped out a message but deleted them all before I could do something stupid like engage in a conversation. Though, now that he was standing on my porch, I saw my error. If I'd texted him back and politely declined one of his many invitations to coffee, I could've avoided this.

Phoenix's brows snapped together, taking him from looking like a six-foot-three wall of pissed-off man to downright sinister.

"You're shitting me," he growled.

I blinked at the harshness of his tone but didn't get a chance to speak—not that I knew how to respond to his bizarre statement—before he went on, "Didn't take you for the type."

Now, wait just a minute. Phoenix didn't know me. I'd had a total of five conversations with him, three of which had taken place at the Hope Center before it had burned down. The first conversation was after Josie Lark, the director of the center, explained to me that Phoenix along with some other men would be volunteering in a big brother sort of program and Josie thought Phoenix would be a good match for Griffin. However, it must be noted during our first meeting Phoenix added very little to the conversation. Only after I agreed to allow Phoenix to spend time with my son did he ask me questions about Griffin. The second and third conversations again revolved around Griff.

And our fourth and fifth meetings couldn't be construed as conversations. The fourth because there had been flames and smoke billowing around us and I barely got out a 'thank you' when Phoenix placed my son on his feet in front of me, then turned and rushed back to the fully engulfed building.

As for the fifth conversation on his doorstep, well, I barely got out a handful of words before I ran.

So it was a definite fact that Phoenix didn't know me, certainly not well enough to make such a bold statement.

Still, I snapped, "What type?"

"The type who doesn't speak her mind."

I had no issue speaking my mind. Actually, I had a hard time keeping my opinions and thoughts to myself. However, I wasn't big on making a fool out of myself. Which was what I'd done showing up at his house.

"How's this for speaking my mind? I'd like you to leave."

"Yeah, I bet you'd like that."

"What's that mean?"

"It means I leave, and you don't have to talk about why the fuck you ran away from me when I told you I'd be right out. It means it'd be easier for you to retreat and not have to explain to me what you thought you were interrupting. Though I can guess."

I felt my cheeks heat and I really hoped they weren't as red as they felt.

"I didn't..." I trailed off because any further words would be a lie. I did run. And I couldn't even argue his point about why I wanted him to leave. So, I settled on, "What do you mean you can guess?"

I shouldn't've asked. It seemed Phoenix, too, didn't lie or sugarcoat the truth to spare someone's feelings.

"You thought I had a woman in my bed. Which makes me wonder why you'd bail knowing I was coming back out to take you somewhere to talk unless you didn't like the thought of me having—"

Oh, no, we weren't going there. That was the only explanation for what came next.

"I left because I was embarrassed."

"Embarrassed?"

"Who are you talking to?" Griff asked from behind me.

I wasn't sure if I was grateful for the interruption or if I wanted a hole to open up and swallow Phoenix Kent out of existence.

Without moving my body, I craned my neck to take in my son from his wild mop of sweaty hair to his dirty t-shirt to his grass-covered jeans. Thankfully, he'd removed his dirty boots before coming in. I was also thankful I hadn't swept because grass clippings now dusted the hardwood floor.

"Officer Kent," I told him.

"Phoenix?"

I couldn't read Griff's tone. There was a lot I couldn't read about my son now that he'd entered his teenage years and had in a blink of an eye gone from my sweet baby boy to a moody man-child. But I did detect some hopefulness mixed in with his normal belligerence.

"Yes, Phoenix."

"What's he doing here?"

Seeing as Griff's face went hard, it wasn't a stretch to deduce I'd been wrong. There was no hope, just hostility.

Unfortunately, since my attention was on my son, Phoenix used this opportunity to enter. This became more regrettable when Griff transferred his gaze from me to Phoenix and narrowed his eyes.

"What are you doing here?" Griff repeated his question.

I jolted at my son's harsh tone.

"Griffin," I warned.

"What?" Griff retorted snottily.

I didn't get a chance to correct my son's disrespect before Phoenix waded in.

"Came by to talk to your mom. Part of what I needed to talk to her about was me taking you to the court so we could play ball."

I wasn't sure if my son was brave or was full of teenage bravado when his eyes remained narrowed and he continued down the path of teenage assholery—something I wasn't a fan of.

"Why would I wanna go anywhere with you?"

The Devil himself could be in my house and I still wouldn't have put up with my son's blatant disrespect. Okay, that was an exaggeration, I'd let Griff slide giving Satan attitude. Anyone else, no freaking way.

"Griffin Cunningham."

My son's gaze sliced to mine, which meant those narrowed eyes landed on me.

"That's not my name!" he shouted and stalked off.

Fuck.

It wasn't even noon and I felt a headache coming on. I lifted my hand, wrapped it around the back of my neck, and squeezed while at the same time I closed my eyes.

I was totally failing.

"Babe?"

I didn't open my eyes. I wasn't ready to face what I created.

"Wren?"

My eyes slowly drifted open but they remained glued to the floor when I spoke.

"I'm not making excuses for his behavior. That was totally unacceptable and out of line. But he's having a rough time with the move. He didn't want to leave Chicago. He had a lot of friends, good ones, and he's pissed at me for making him leave his life."

And he was pissed at his father. Not that Conor had been much of a dad, but he had come around occasionally and when he did, he was a weekend-fun-time dad. Meaning that the four times a year Conor remembered he had a son, he spoiled Griff in an effort to make up for all the other times he didn't. Now Conor was gone for good, and my son was struggling with that, too.

"What'd Griff mean when he said that wasn't his real name?"

Something else my son wasn't happy about—the name change.

I wasn't sure what came over me—maybe I wanted to shock the beautiful Officer Kent. Maybe I wanted to burn the bridge so thoroughly Phoenix would leave and never come back. Maybe I was just being a bitch because I was having a bad day.

No, I was having a bad freaking decade.

"When my ex-husband got sentenced to life for murder one, I changed Griff's last name to my maiden name."

I'd changed mine before the ink was dry on my divorce decree ten years ago, but as shitty of a father as Conor was, I'd stupidly held out hope he'd one day come around and be the man Griff needed him to be, so I didn't push for Griff's name to be changed. Hindsight being what it was, I should've changed my son's last name and run. I should've taken my sweet boy and kept him far away from my piece of shit ex.

I heard Phoenix suck in a breath. Internally I smiled. I knew when I looked up, I'd find disgust and revulsion. I needed that. I needed Phoenix to leave and never come back.

"The center's not gonna be open for another few months," he started. "I don't think it'd be a good idea to wait that long for me to spend time with Griff."

The speed in which my eyes shot to Phoenix made me momentarily dizzy and when my vision cleared, I did not see disgust and revulsion.

I saw pain and not a small amount of it.

So much pain it leaked from his pores.

It filled my house and pressed against my chest.

"What?" I wheezed.

"I can't come around every day because of work," he went on as if I hadn't coughed out a question. "Two, three times a week I'll swing by after he gets home from school. We'll adjust if we need to."

"Swing by?"

He continued ignoring me.

"That means you're gonna have to pick up the phone when I call. In my line of work, shit comes up at the last minute. Which isn't ideal when I'm trying to build trust, but I'll talk to Griff and explain it to him. He's smart, he'll understand the difference."

"The difference about what?"

"Between an asshole who makes plans and doesn't show up and a man who is a cop and can't control when criminals decide to be criminals. It might take a minute, but he'll know when I make a promise, I keep it. So when I make plans to be here after school to pick him up, I'll be here, and the only reason why I'd need to reschedule is if I'm caught up at work. In which case, we'll reschedule."

What was happening?

How was this happening?

"Phoenix—"

"You need to answer your phone when I call," he reiterated. "And you need to tell Griff he needs to answer my texts."

Wait.

"You have Griff's number?"

"Yep. And like his mother, he has been ignoring my calls and texts. Another reason for today's visit. I'm done with that. I gave him time; I see I shouldn't've. I thought seeing me too soon after the fire would cause him harm. But before that shit went down, we were finally connecting."

I was busy trying to stop my legs from giving out and my head from spinning at this new information, so I missed Phoenix moving closer to me.

But I didn't miss him invading my space, nor did I miss the way his hand came up to cup my cheek. And when he spoke, his words worked their way over my skin and heated me from the inside out.

"Two things. There was no woman in my bed. I pulled a double and was sleeping." I'd barely comprehended what he said before he decimated my good sense. "And I didn't invite you in because me and you alone in my apartment isn't a good idea."

"Why not?"

That was when the mask Phoenix Kent wore fell away and I got my first look at his unguarded features. Agony so stark it couldn't be described as pain. It was more, so much more. Looking at Phoenix, only one word came to mind —*shattered*.

His soul was in tatters.

But instead of playing it smart and retreating to a place of safety I reached up and covered his hand with mine.

Then I did something I hadn't done in over ten years; I showed myself.

The real me.

The broken, frayed, pieced-back-together woman.

The failure.

I knew he saw it when his blue eyes sparked with fire.

"That right there, is why you're not safe around me," he whispered before he let his hand fall away, taking mine with it. "I'll be in touch."

He was at the door preparing to leave and I knew I should've let it go, but I couldn't. I had to know.

"Why am I not safe around you?"

When he spoke, I was grateful I was staring at his back.

"You know why, Wren. You and I, we're the same. I see you the same as you see me. The problem is you're stronger than I am and if you turn that iron will my way and push, I'll cave. I won't stand a chance and that's dangerous. I'm broken in a way that will last a lifetime and you got a boy to look after. So, I need to keep space between us. I definitely don't need to be alone with you in my apartment."

With that, he stepped out onto the porch and closed the door behind him.

I stood there long after he was gone staring at that closed door doing everything I could to strengthen my resolve to heed Phoenix's warning.

Once I shored up my determination, I went in search of my teenage son who needed a reminder in manners and respect.

2

I tossed my bag on my sofa and looked around my filthy apartment noting the glaring difference between what was only a step up from a crash pad and the home Wren had created for her son.

The kid had no idea how lucky he was. I barely remembered what it was like to have a mother and I grew up in a shithole that was only slightly more disgusting than the current state of my apartment.

I needed a cleaning service. Now that my sister was shacked up with her fiancé Luke, my older brother River had moved to Idaho, and my eldest brother Echo was brooding over a woman he let slip away I had no reason to clean. Sad but true. My siblings were the only ones I allowed to enter my apartment and since they were all occupied or out of state, I'd let my apartment turn to shit. I blamed my aversion to cleaning on Echo. After our dad went down for murder and Echo fully took over, he made us clean constantly. The house was a shithole, in a shit part of town, but the inside was spotless.

Just like Wren's home.

I moved through the living area into the kitchen and bent to grab a black Hefty bag from under the sink. I opened the bag and without looking—I didn't need to, it was all garbage—I swept the shit littering the countertops into the bag. When I was done in the kitchen, I moved back into the living room and cleared the coffee table of the pizza box and to-go cups. From there I went to the small dining room table and did the same.

I was tying up the bag trying to remember if I still owned a vacuum cleaner when a knock on my door saved me from admitting I did, I just hadn't used it in years.

Christ, I'm a slob.

"Who is it?" I called out.

"Griffin."

Irrational fear licked up my spine as I rushed to the door. Call it an occupational hazard; I knew better than most the bad shit that happened. And since there was no reason for Griffin to be at my apartment in the middle of the afternoon and I didn't know how he made it from his house to mine, my mind jumped to the worst-case scenario.

I unlocked and swung the door open, then looked the kid over from his baseball hat to his sneakers.

"You okay?" I asked.

Without preamble, he launched right in, "Why'd you come to the house?"

I stepped aside and motioned for him to enter.

The kid ignored my invitation.

Fuck, it was uncanny. It was like looking back in time and staring at myself.

"I'll answer that when you tell me how you got here and if your mom knows you're here."

"I walked."

"Right. Come in and we'll talk."

I needed to text Wren and tell her Griff was at my house and not in school where he was supposed to be.

"I don't want to play ball with you," he spat.

Oh, yeah, fuck yeah, it was like looking in a mirror. All that pent-up frustration. The need to have control over something but not understanding why, so you did the only thing you could do to control your surroundings and pushed everyone away.

"Alright, Griff, we won't play ball. Though without practice you won't reach your full potential."

"So? Mom's gonna make me quit the team when report cards come out."

Fuck. He was failing his classes.

Wren was going to rightly hit the roof.

"Not smart fucking off school."

Griff shrugged and did his best to pretend he didn't care.

"Whatever. I came by to tell you I don't need a babysitter, so you don't need to call my mom."

In the weeks I'd spent time with Griffin I'd tried the nice guy routine with him, and it had gotten me nowhere. And to say that was a difficult task to accomplish when a smart-mouthed teenager was dishing out shit would be an understatement. I didn't have a dad who was good or loving, I had a dickhead who doled out punishment with his fists. I would never understand a man who took his hand to his child in anger intending to do damage. But I understood how raising a teenage boy would try the patience of a saint and I'd only spent a handful of hours with the kid.

It was time to switch it up and give the kid some honesty—something I had a feeling no man in his life had ever given him.

"That's not why you're here," I shot back.

"Yes, it—"

"You did not cut class and walk, what, ten miles to get here to tell me you don't need a babysitter. You have a phone, and you have my number. You could've texted me that you didn't want to play ball. You're here because you're pissed at me. So man up and speak your mind. No bullshit. No hiding. Tell me what's on your mind. We'll talk it through, then I'll drive you back to school."

The kid said nothing, though he got points for keeping a straight face while he held my stare.

"We can do this all day, friend. I got nowhere to be. But I'm dead-ass tired after working a twelve-hour shift and I just got home. So if you wanna continue this tough guy stare down you're gonna have to do it from the couch because my ass is sitting down."

I didn't wait for his reply. I turned, leaving him standing in the hall, went to my couch, and sat.

It took longer than I thought it would before he came in and slammed the door.

"Feel better?" I asked.

"What?"

"Slamming the door, disrupting my neighbors, did it make you feel better? Because I have to say, that's a weak move. A real man keeps his anger in check. He certainly doesn't disrespect property that's not his."

To his credit, he didn't bother denying or arguing about the door. He simply shrugged his backpack off and sat on the couch.

"Why'd you come by my house?" he asked.

"I told you why. I had some stuff to clear up with your mom and I'd waited long enough to reconnect with you."

"Why'd you wait?"

Fuck.

I shouldn't've waited.

I was contemplating how much to tell him when I came to the conclusion that he wasn't the kid I thought he was. He was fourteen. He was also a fourteen-year-old without a father. He had a good mom who cared but his dad went down for murder one and damn if I didn't know what that was like. I also remembered what it was like when Echo tried to cushion every bump so I wouldn't feel any more shit. I didn't appreciate being treated like I was fragile.

"I waited because after the fire I thought you needed time before I started coming around. I didn't want you seeing me to bring back bad shit. Something like that can screw with your head and I didn't want to be the cause of any more trauma for you."

"So you let me..." he trailed off.

"I let you what?"

"Go through the bad shit by myself," he hissed. "You were there, then you weren't. You told me you'd be there, and you lied."

Jesus fuck. My chest burned with regret. I was a total asshole. During the fire, while we were stuck in the locker room, I had told Griff I wouldn't leave him. However, I told him that when he thought I was going to leave him in a burning building.

"Griffin, I did not leave you," I reminded him. "Not then and not now. I was wrong, but I thought I was doing right by letting you have time to settle before I started coming around again."

"Well, now I don't want you around anymore."

I'd heard that before. When I first started going to the Hope Center to volunteer, Griff had made it clear he didn't want me around. It had taken me a week to get him to stop scowling and being a pain in the ass. And since I'd royally fucked up it would seem we were back to that.

"I don't believe you."

"You're calling me a liar?"

Christ, this kid's attitude.

"Again, you didn't walk ten miles to tell me you don't want me around. I get why you're pissed. I screwed up. I admit it. I see now I should not have given you time. I should've been at your house the next day. But just to add, I was also giving your mom some space. The last she saw of me I was carrying the most precious thing in her life out of a burning building. You were covered in soot and soaking wet. She was scared out of her mind. Seeing me would've been a reminder of the fire and it would've put her right back there, standing outside watching the flames eat that building and not knowing what was going on inside. But you and I, we lived a different kind of scared, we were in the thick of it. I'm sorry, Griffin, I didn't—"

"You were scared?"

"Fuck yeah, I was scared. We were trapped in a fire."

Griffin's face finally cracked. Gone was the pretense of an uncaring teenager. He was staring at me with a mixture of disbelief and relief.

"My mom had nightmares," he mumbled.

I felt that spear through my heart.

More hurt she covered up.

"Do you?"

"Sometimes," he admitted. "But not bad ones like her. I just dream about you running out."

"I would *never* run out on you." Griff jolted and maybe I should've felt bad for startling the kid, but he had to understand. "I would *never* leave you in a goddamn burning building to die alone."

His posture stiffened and his shoulders jerked up damn near to his ears when he clarified, "You're running out of the building carrying me. That's what I dream about."

It was my turn to stiffen and when I did, I felt every muscle tense.

"Griff—"

"You didn't leave me," he whispered. "But then you did."

Fucking hell.

"Can you maybe try to understand I didn't leave you, and while I see now I was wrong, I was trying to do right by you and your mom?"

"I don't know."

Well, at least that was honest.

"So what do we do now?" I asked.

"I don't know."

I glanced down at my watch. Seeing as it was nearing three, either school was out, or it was getting ready to dismiss for the day, so there was no sense in me driving him back there.

"What time does your mom get done with work?"

"Five. But she doesn't get home until six."

"Right. So you're hanging out here with me until your mom's home."

His face went straight back to defiant teenager.

"I don't need a babysitter."

"That's debatable since you skipped school and you're failing your classes. But I'm not here to babysit you. Since you came by and interrupted me cleaning, you're gonna help me, then I'm gonna take you home."

Griff glanced around my apartment and when his gaze came back to mine, he was frowning.

"Dude, it doesn't look like this place has been cleaned in a year."

"You'd be right."

"I can walk home."

If I'd been him, I'd've opted to walk the ten miles home, too.

"You're vacuuming."

"I vacuumed yesterday," he complained.

"Great, then you know how to do it."

His brows shot up and he asked, "You don't?"

"From the time I was younger than you until I moved out on my own my brother made me vacuum twice a week. My older brother River had two days and my sister Shiloh had two days. Echo got one day but that's only because he was in charge of cooking. When River moved out, Shiloh and I each got an extra day."

"Your brother made you? Not your mom?"

Normally I would deflect. I didn't speak about the woman who gave birth to me and then callously tossed me and my siblings away. But I had a relationship to mend, an important one that I'd destroyed.

"I didn't have a mom. She left when I was a kid."

Griffin's eyes rounded and his frown deepened.

"Why'd she leave?"

Now that was a question I wasn't prepared to answer.

"Hell if I know."

"I'm...um...sorry you don't have a mom."

I tried to think if anyone had ever said that to me before.

But since I made a religion out of avoiding any talk about her, I reckoned no one ever had. And it was weird hearing Griff say it.

I didn't have a mom.

But I did, she just didn't want me.

3

I was fuming mad.
So freaking mad, I was near tears as I drove home from work.

In the hours since Phoenix texted me to tell me my son had skipped school and walked to his apartment, I had not calmed down. I wasn't sure which I was most pissed about, my son cutting school, or Griff walking across town to Phoenix's, or that just two days after he'd shown up at my house, I had to face him again, or that Griffin was failing two classes.

Okay, I was sure. I was pissed about *all* of it.

No, I was furious.

It was times like these when I was at a loss of what to do, how to react, and what the appropriate response should be that I hated my parents. I hated that my father was a liar and my mother was a bitch and neither of them taught me anything in life. Well, they taught me who I didn't want to be but in times like these that didn't help much. All I knew was that screaming at the top of my lungs wouldn't work because it never worked on me. Taking away all of my son's electronics didn't work because I'd already tried that, and he was still acting like a jerk. Giving him more chores didn't work either.

I'd read books and blogs, watched parenting videos on YouTube, and still, I had no clue what the hell to do with my kid.

At this point, I wasn't sure who needed the straitjacket, me or him or both of us.

And the worst part was I had no one to call. I didn't have a single person I could reach out to and ask for advice. There was no one to vent to. No one to co-parent with.

Just, no one.

By the time I pulled onto my street I was no less angry, but anxiety had crept in. The terrifying realization that I could very seriously be screwing up my kid in ways that he wouldn't come back from. That *we* couldn't come back from.

Hurt people hurt people.

Was that what I was doing?

Was I unintentionally hurting my boy? Were all my bad life choices catching up with me? I left Chicago to give Griffin a fresh start. I changed his last name so he wouldn't be tied to a man who was a convicted murderer. I moved so he could make new friends and not have people treat him like the son of a felon.

Or did I take my son from his home so *I* wouldn't have to face the backlash? Did I rip my son away from his friends, his teachers, and his hometown so I could have a fresh start and not be the ex-wife of Conor Masterson?

With a thousand thoughts racing, including what I was going to make for dinner—the least taxing of my evening's agenda—I hitched my purse over my shoulder and made my way through my garage. I scooted around the boxes I had yet to unpack, sidestepped Griff's bike which he had yet to ride since we moved to Georgia and opened the door.

Then I stopped dead.

One of the things I loved about the new house was the attached garage. I also loved the big laundry room slash mud room when I came in from the garage, which led into the kitchen with a big island. Around the corner was a large dining room that flowed into the living room. Between the dining and living areas, the wall opened to a long hallway which three bedrooms sprouted from along with a guest bathroom.

And right then I had a clear view of Phoenix at the kitchen sink.

His head turned in my direction. Pot of steaming water held aloft, his eyes met mine.

Cold and distant.

Neither of us said a word, not for long moments. Then slowly the hardness that normally suffused his features softened. It wasn't the same as what he gave me the other day—he was still safely behind his wall—but some of the coldness warmed.

Without a word, he went back to work straining spaghetti noodles.

Belatedly the smell of garlic and parsley hit me. I couldn't remember a time I'd ever walked into my house after work, or any other time besides, and smelled food cooking.

"I don't understand why I have to learn about the Pythagorean Theorem." I heard Griff complain though I couldn't see him.

Phoenix didn't miss a beat when he answered, "You need to know it if you want to be an engineer, or an architect, or if you want to survey mountains, or if you want to go into the security field."

"Security field?"

"I won't pretend to understand but I've heard my sister's fiancé Luke talking about it with Dylan when they're drawing up schematics for a security system. Something to do with the angles of the cameras and field of vision. But just to add, even if you want to be a mechanic you still need to know it so you can pass math."

"Do you know what the Pythagorean Theorem is?"

I was surprised this question wasn't asked with attitude; Griff merely sounded curious.

"Nope. But I was a straight-A student, so I reckon I knew what it was in ninth grade."

Phoenix was a straight-A student?

I had yet to recover from that tidbit of information or from the smell of garlic and parsley or from the weird albeit wonderful conversation Phoenix was having with Griff when Phoenix finished with the noodles and went back to the stove.

"Babe, you gonna stand there all night?"

I didn't answer because I was thinking I just might stand there all night if it meant I got a few minutes of listening to Griff sounding like his old self. Not to mention, I'd never heard my son asking anyone but me about his homework. Which brought up the fact he was doing his homework and I wasn't the one who had to harp on him to sit down. So, yes, I was going to stand there all night so as not to break whatever spell had been cast over my house.

Phoenix tipped his head in my direction and openly studied me.

I liked his eyes on me.

I liked him in my kitchen.

I liked him chatting with my son while he was making dinner.

I'll cave.

Damn, I really wanted Phoenix to cave. I wanted to know what pained him. I wanted to know if he played football or basketball in high school. I wanted to know about his family. I wanted to know everything about him. And as inappropriate as it was with my son in the other room, I wanted to know what those hands would feel like on my skin. I wanted to feel the weight of him blanketing me as he moved inside of me. I wanted to taste his lips and other places besides. I wanted to know if his chest felt as hard as it looked. I wanted to trace his tattoos with my tongue.

I had to snap out of it. I had to play this smart. Not only for me but for Griff.

"Seriously, Wren, dinner's almost done."

Dinner was almost done.

A dinner I hadn't made.

A meal that Phoenix had cooked in my kitchen.

Yep, I needed to shove my unwelcome thoughts into a box and mark it Do Not Open.

I didn't trust myself to form words, too afraid I'd blurt out the truth, so I nodded and took a few tentative steps. When I got close, Phoenix's hand shot out and wrapped around my wrist. Once again, I felt the spark of electricity. The desire that sizzled from nothing more than a simple touch.

"You okay?" he asked quietly.

"No."

"Babe." That was infinitely softer.

And because it was and he'd been honest with me, I thought I'd return the favor.

"I appreciate what you did today with Griff and bringing

him home. But this..." I paused and tipped my head to the pot of spaghetti sauce on the stove. "Isn't smart."

The blue of Phoenix's eyes deepened.

I didn't have to say more—he knew.

"Wren—"

"I'm not strong, Phoenix. The other day you gave it to me straight, so consider this your warning. I'll push. I'll want more of this. I'll dig in because that's who I am. You were right, we are the same and it's not smart. Especially because something is going on with my son. I need all my energy focused on him, not guarding my stupid heart against falling for a man who very honestly told me he was broken in a way that would never be fixed. And I'd try. I'd work hard at it. I'd want to stop your pain because I know what it feels like to live with it day in and day out, eating away at your insides. And I don't want that for you."

That stupid heart of mine flip-flopped when he loosened his hand around my wrist just a skoosh and his thumb pressed against the inside tendon there. I vaguely wondered if he could feel my pulse racing. I not so vaguely understood that I needed this to end. I could no longer endure his proximity or those beautiful eyes staring into mine. I could no longer withstand what they said and what I knew he was reading from me.

"I feel you, baby. Go get changed. We'll eat, and then before you talk to Griff, you and I need to have a conversation. Then I'll leave you to your night."

Baby.

Lawd God, he was torturing me.

"Okay."

He let go of my wrist and the cold settled back into his features.

I walked through my kitchen wondering if anyone else

saw the difference. Or better yet, if Phoenix allowed anyone to see the depth of his agony.

I found Griff sitting at the formal dining room table we never used with his book open and a notebook in front of him. When he caught sight of me his face bleached of color and looked contrite.

This was how he got away with more than he should have. That look of remorse. The sweetness in his expression that reminded me of when he was younger.

But I was doing him no favors by going easy on him when he screwed up.

"Mom—"

"Not yet, son." I watched Griff swallow. "Something for you to think about before we talk, and, Griff, I need you to take this seriously and think hard because tonight you're gonna talk and I'm gonna listen. Tonight's your night to lay it all out, everything you think I've done wrong, I'm doing wrong, things I'm messing up. Nothing's off limits. Complete honesty."

"I don't—"

"Not yet. Think about it."

My boy who was no longer a little boy but not yet a man, stuck in this strange and scary place between adolescence and maturity, slid his eyes back to his notebook.

"I'll think about it," he mumbled.

I didn't ask about his homework even though I was dying to. I simply left it there and continued on to my bedroom. Griffin's bedroom door was closed, and I was dying to open it and check if he'd put away his laundry like he was supposed to do when he got home from school. Which of course was doubtful since he'd spent the afternoon at Phoenix's. But I wasn't going to think about that, either. Not about Phoenix taking care of a mess that was not his, and not about my son seeking out a man he barely knew to have a conversation about something I wasn't privy to. I was hoping this discussion Phoenix wanted to have after dinner would include him telling me why my kid walked ten freaking miles to talk to him instead of calling him on the phone.

And I had more questions like how my son knew where Phoenix lived. He wasn't listed; I knew because I'd looked. Josie had given me his address and only because she knew I needed to thank him in person for saving Griff. That wasn't something you did over the phone.

With a thousand thoughts tumbling in my mind, I quickly discarded my work clothes. But instead of putting on my ratty-assed sweats and t-shirt like I normally did, I grabbed my favorite pair of jeans that did wonders for my behind and ignored the tiny voice in the back of my mind that told me I was stupid. I ignored it again when I pulled a cute flowy top off a hanger. I also didn't think about why I went into my bathroom to check my hair and brush my teeth.

And since I was in complete denial about my behavior, I didn't think about how ridiculously anxious I was. So with minty fresh breath and a cute outfit, I made my way back down the hall while wondering how I was going to survive dinner with Phoenix. I hadn't yet puzzled that out when I stopped dead at the mouth of the hall. From there I could see the back of my son still sitting in the chair, Phoenix at his side with one hand on the top rung of the ladderback chair and the other flat on the table. He was leaning in close to Griff. My breath was arrested and a burn that started in my chest spread like wildfire.

I stood frozen as the sight before me blistered my retinas.

An image so beautiful it hurt.

An image that was a mirage.

I shifted my eyes from Phoenix helping my son with his homework to the stack of plates on the table. Yes, this was a beautiful illusion, one that was not and never would be our life.

Phoenix's head turned and my gaze skidded back to him. When our eyes locked, another agonizing stab pierced straight through my heart.

Straight. Through.

So deep, I was wondering if the tip of the blade had nicked my soul.

I wanted to latch onto the moment, live in it, bask in the beauty of Phoenix being in my house helping my son, giving the moment to Griffin. But I had to play this smart, keep me and Griff safely behind the wall I'd erected around us. I knew this, yet I couldn't find it in me to break the spell.

Thankfully Phoenix could, but I had a feeling it was only because there was a knock at the door. His brows pulled together slightly before he looked over my shoulder.

He straightened to his full height while asking, "Expecting company?"

Before I could answer, Griff shifted in his chair and his head tipped to the side as he took me in. Notwithstanding my boy's current GPA the universe had blessed me with a highly intelligent kid. Therefore, he was clever enough to suss out why I hadn't changed into kickback clothes. Not that I'd wear ratty-assed sweats when there was company of any kind over for dinner, however, I did have more comfortable clothes I could've changed into.

I watched Griff roll his eyes and decided since I was already ignoring my behavior, I would ignore his observations and opt to answer Phoenix's question instead.

"No, I'm not expecting company."

I started toward the door and, much like the other day, I did this contemplating my lack of friends. It was high time I stopped being closed off and made some. If not for me, for Griff. He needed to see me settling. I also mentally scolded myself for not making the time to buy a new front door that had a peephole or some windows. It wasn't safe for a woman living alone not to know who was on the other side of the door before she opened it. And, in my opinion, calling out "who is it" was rude, so I didn't do that.

Consequently, I came face-to-face with a man I never thought I'd see again.

No, a man I never *wanted* to see again.

In my shock and panic, I did not do what I should've done, which was slam the door in my ex-husband's attorney's face. Instead, I stood immobile, not understanding how Bill Carry had found me. I'd been careful—extra careful. I was not listed on any online people searches. I was studious about checking and had spent hours opting out of every site when I first moved to Georgia. I had a post office box. Griffin's school registration was void of our home address—I'd begged the principal who had to get it okayed by the school superintendent and they finally agreed to allow me to use the PO box.

That meant it had taken Bill time to find me. He'd had to dig deep, which said not good things about why he'd seek me out.

"Wren—"

"What are you doing here, Bill?"

I had to hand it to the guy; he tried to cover up his irritation. However, growing up the way I did, always watching and waiting for the explosion of anger, I didn't miss the tic in his cheek, or the tightness around his eyes.

He was not happy he'd had to waste time finding me and he was unhappy I wasn't asking him in like an old friend. Though I couldn't imagine why he thought I'd allow him into my home after our not-so-pleasant farewell after Conor's sentencing. I'd only gone to make sure the bastard got the punishment he deserved.

"You moved..." Bill's gaze shot over my shoulder, his eyes widened to an unnatural size, and he jerked back. What he didn't do was finish his statement.

"Is there a problem?" That came from Phoenix in a not-to-be-mistaken gruff tone that clearly conveyed there'd better not be a problem. And if there was, there wouldn't be one for long.

Bill's slimy eyes were still wide when they slid back to me. I wasn't happy to have his attention back. I was seriously embarrassed Phoenix was there to witness how this scene was going to play out and horrified Griff was within earshot. But I was more than ecstatic that the color had bleached from Bill's face at the sight of Phoenix.

"Can we please speak in private?"

"As I told you the last time I saw you, I have nothing further to say to you."

"Conor's trying to get in touch." Bill told me something I very well knew since the letters he'd been sending to my old address had been forwarded to my post office box. I just hadn't opened any of them which meant I obviously hadn't responded.

"As I told him the last time I spoke to him, I have nothing to say to him either. And you know that since you were there."

"Griffin is his son."

I felt it start—the fury in my stomach that would turn to acid if I allowed it. The rage and anger that would consume me. The overwhelming urge a mama has to maim when her baby is being threatened.

Biology would agree Griffin was Conor's son. But at no point had Conor been a real dad to my son. At no point had Conor cared more about his son than his own selfish needs. At no fucking point in the last fourteen years had Conor stopped to wonder how his actions would affect his son. And finally, Griffin was not Conor's priority when he shot and killed a man and was condemned to life in prison.

Fuck Conor.

And fuck Bill.

"Leave," I seethed. "And do not come back. This is your one warning, Bill. The next time I hear from you I'm reporting it to the police and filing for a restraining order."

"Conor needs—"

"Wren's asked you to leave so it's time you do that," Phoenix interrupted.

"Who are you?"

"For the purpose of this conversation, I'm a friend of Wren's. If in five seconds you're not gone, I will be the cop who escorts you off the property."

Bill's posture changed when he spat, "Cop?"

"You can tell my dad we don't want his money," Griff announced.

Um, what?

I spun around and this was unfortunate as it meant I ran smack dab into Phoenix. Before I could fall, his hand shot out and he pulled me tight against his chest. He shuffled us to the side and without turning his back to Bill, he made it so I could see my son.

"That's why you're here, right?" Griff continued with his arms crossed over his chest. "Well, you can report back to *Conor* we don't want anything from him."

"Griffin, son—"

"Fuck you, I'm not your son!" my boy shouted, and I jolted.

Phoenix didn't jolt. His body slowly went from stiff to stone.

"Baby, go to Griff." Phoenix let me go and when I didn't move right away, he gave me a gentle shove and repeated, "Go to Griff. I'll handle this."

At this point, I had no option but to go to my son because Phoenix was prowling toward Bill, and with the hostility rolling off of him, I was afraid of what he might do and what Griff might see.

Perhaps a better person would've put some effort into calming down the pissed-off giant who could snap average-sized Bill in half. I, however, was not a better person, and right then with Griff shaking in fury and it being Bill who had made him that way on top of everything else that asshole had done, I didn't give two shits if Phoenix tore him apart.

I didn't make it to Griff before I heard the door slam. My son's hands came up in a conciliatory gesture that did not one thing to assuage my worry and anger.

"Okay, Mom, don't be mad," he rushed out.

Too late, I was furious. I just didn't know how mad I should've been at my son.

"Griff—"

"I read the letters," he said over me. "I know I shouldn't've but I needed to know."

He read Conor's letters.

Oh, shit.

The anger slid away and pain bloomed in my heart. So much pain I couldn't speak through it.

Griffin didn't have the same dilemma.

"I know why you didn't tell me about them. You think I can't handle it. You also think I don't know why we have a PO box when we have a mailbox right in front of our freaking house."

I heard the door open. Griff's gaze flicked that way, but he didn't stop raging. "You treat me like I'm five. I *know* what he did, Mom. Hell, everyone knows what he did. You can't protect me from it and moving to Georgia isn't going to change who I am. Bill is right." Griffin's face twisted in disgust as he spat out, "I'm his son."

With that, I found my voice.

"Your father made bad choices but that doesn't—"

Griffin leaned in and shouted, "Stop defending him!"

"No."

One rumbled word from Phoenix.

Shit.

"She doesn't need to defend that piece of shit," Griff spat. "He's a murderer."

He was right, his father was a piece-of-shit murderer, and as much as it pained me down to the deepest depths of my soul, I promised myself I would never be like my parents and talk trash about the other. I would never turn into my mother and tell my son all of his father's shortcomings. I wouldn't be like my father and call Conor names to Griffin. That didn't mean I didn't think Conor wasn't a lowdown bastard, but I would never say it to my son.

"I get that you're pissed right now, but you do not yell at your mother," Phoenix said like it was a commandment set in stone.

"You have no idea," Griff hissed. "You have no idea what it's like. Everyone knows. Every. One. My mom couldn't get away from it. Everyone talking shit about her behind her back. Both of us getting looks everywhere we went. My mom had to quit her job. I lost all my friends. We lost everything because he's a deadbeat, piece-of-shit *murderer,* and she defends him."

I felt wet hit my eyes, the kind that no amount of blinking was going to stop from spilling over as my heart once again shattered for my son.

Yep.

I was totally failing.

"I'm not defending him. He took a man's life and he's paying for that. What I won't do is participate in talking badly—"

"Why not? Maybe that's what I need. Maybe I want my mom to be just as mad as me. Maybe I need to hear you tell me he's a worthless asshole. Maybe I need you to stop acting like I'm a kid and start treating me like I'm almost grown."

Under the circumstances, I figured the level of hate I felt for my ex-husband was natural. At first, I'd let it consume me, but slowly I healed from his deceit only to watch him break Griff's heart over and over. The hatred I'd felt had turned into revulsion and stayed that way until Conor killed a man in cold blood. Then that revulsion turned into something more. Something so huge I couldn't give a name to the feeling. But standing in my living room, looking at my beautiful son vibrating with anger, shaking with emotions he couldn't understand, I knew what I felt for Conor—utter disgust.

Loathing.

Violence.

Years and years of suppressed anger I could no longer keep a lid on.

This was one of those times when I should've taken a breath. I should've counted to ten and remembered I was a mother, and even though I wasn't doing a great job at the moment, I tried to be a good one. I should've done a lot of things differently. But right then my vision hazed, and I turned into everything I never wanted to be—my mother.

"You wanna know how mad I am, Griff? You wanna know how much I hate him? You wanna know that there were days after I left him when I couldn't get out of bed because I was so broken? You wanna know how many times I cried myself to sleep after I held you for hours and hours after he didn't show up? I hate him for what he's done to you. I will die hating him. He is exactly what you say he is— a piece-of-shit father I could not protect you from. I hate him for that. I am so goddamn angry I couldn't shield you from the shit he dumped on us. I hate that I had to move us. I hate that you know we're hiding. I hate that you found those letters and read them. I hate that there is nothing I can do to protect my boy from a man who's such an asshole he has the nerve to try and contact us. But I cannot and never will hate the man he was when he gave me you. So when you think I'm defending him, what I'm really doing is trying to remind myself that once my son's father had some good in him."

"Finally." Griff threw his arms in the air. "You wanted me to lay it out, so here it is. I'm pissed at you for lying to me when all you do is preach about being honest."

My son's accusation slammed into me and took my breath.

"I don't lie—"

"You do. Every day when you pretend you're not sad. You think I don't see it? You think that I didn't know that you've been alone all these years because of what he did to you? I'm pissed at you because you think I don't know. I'm pissed because there is nothing I can do to make it better for you when you bust your ass every day to try and make it better for me."

"Easy," Phoenix murmured.

I jolted at the sound of his voice. I'd forgotten he was in the room.

"Mom—"

"No, son," I quickly cut in. "You're right. I asked you to be honest with me. And I guess..." I had to stop to swallow down the boulder that had taken purchase in my throat. "I can see why you think I've been lying to you. I'm sad about a lot of things. However, none of those things have to do with you and I need you to get that. I love you, Griff, more than anything else in the world, love you. I also need you to understand I didn't move us here to get away from people talking trash about me. I did it so you wouldn't have to hear it. I did it so you could be you and not Conor Masterson's son. That's also why I changed your name. I should've asked you about that and I'm sorry I didn't. But, Griff, we have to see our way outta the anger. We have to work together; I can't do this alone. As far as treating you like a kid, well, if you want me to stop doing that I need you to show me you can act like a young man."

Some of the annoyance drained out of his features but he was hanging on to his anger.

"I can't see my way out of it," he admitted.

Freaking finally, I was getting somewhere with him.

"Then let's work on that, yeah?"

"Yeah, whatever."

"Not whatever. I need you to work with me. We have to find a way to move on from this. Together."

"Are *you* gonna work on moving on?" The gentle tone my boy used changed the question from sounding like a smart-mouthed quip to genuine concern.

So with that hanging in the air, I gave the only answer I could.

"Yes, Griff, I'll work on moving on."

No sooner had the words left my mouth than I was praying I was telling the truth.

"Promise?"

Shit.

"Promise."

Griff nodded. "Then I'll work on moving on."

Even though I knew he wasn't fully committed to working on anything I still felt relief. I knew it was going to take more than a heated discussion to heal what had been broken.

But it was a start.

"Can we eat now? I'm starving."

I bet he was after all of the exercise he had skipping school and walking to Phoenix's.

Before I could answer, Phoenix did. "Clean up your homework, bud, and I'll get the food on the table."

A weird sensation traveled through me. I couldn't place the feeling except to say that it wasn't entirely unwelcome. It was strange and scary, yet warm and comforting.

Griff turned to pick up his books off the table and when I made my move to follow, Phoenix's hand circled my wrist.

"You okay?"

Without looking at him I nodded.

"No, Wren, are you okay?"

The softness in his voice made me turn my attention to him and the moment I did I regretted it.

Unfiltered.

Exposed.

The real, unmasked Phoenix with all of his pain shining from his beautiful blue eyes.

And since Griff was right about me preaching honesty, I gave it to Phoenix.

"I'll never be okay."

Apparently, Phoenix subscribed to my way of thinking. All he did was dip his chin in understanding. After all, he knew, since he was broken in a way that would last until his final breath.

We were the same.

4

I needed to get the fuck out of Wren's house.
It was too hard to breathe, too hard to think, too fucking hard to look at Griff.

You have no idea.

Griffin's mistaken assumption replayed in my head on repeat. Over and over, I heard the kid's scratchy voice and wondered if that was what I sounded like when I argued with my brother about our father. Had my voice wobbled with pain? Had it pitched high with anger?

Jesus fucking hell, I needed to leave.

My skin itched as glimpses of my childhood flashed in my mind. Sparks of memories I didn't want to remember. Shit that I'd worked hard to bury and forget. I'd made it so the first seventeen years of my life were wiped clean from my brain.

That was, until now.

Now I couldn't shove it back. I couldn't watch Griff— listen to him, see the agony rip through him—and not feel, not remember, not taste the desperation of a young man trying to figure things out.

Wren was his Echo.

The touchstone. The provider. The voice of reason in all the noise. Like my brother, she'd work herself to the bone to help her son. And like my brother she'd mostly fail. Not because she didn't love her boy. Not because she wasn't trying hard enough. Because like Echo she was trying too hard to make everything okay when it absolutely wasn't.

I glanced across the table at Wren and watched as she slowly twirled her spaghetti around her fork. She was trying her best but doing a shit job of hiding her worry. Griff on the other hand was having no problem shoveling his food in his mouth while simultaneously hiding his anger.

"Have you ever had to kill anyone?" Griff asked around a mouthful.

Wren came out of her hunch and her gaze slid to her boy. Before she could reprimand the kid, I answered, "Once."

Without missing a beat Griff went on, "Ever been shot at?"

"Yep."

Beautiful, startled blue eyes hit mine and I waited for Griff to continue.

He didn't disappoint with his follow-up, "What's that like?"

"Not fun."

"Did you shoot back?"

I watched as the tension inched its way over Wren's pretty features. The current topic of discussion wasn't something I wanted to discuss; however, it was better than thinking about my shit father, or Griff's.

"Yep."

"Why'd you wanna be a cop?"

Fuck.

Motherfuck.

It was no secret why I'd become a cop. Anyone who'd lived in the area long enough knew who Lester Kent was, knew what he did, and knew who his children were. But Wren and Griff hadn't lived in the area for long so they had no clue why Echo pushed us all to go into law enforcement.

"My brothers are cops and so is my sister."

I was well aware I'd choked out my answer, so when Wren's stare became reflective it wasn't a surprise.

"What about your dad? Is he a cop, too?"

Jesus Christ, I couldn't breathe.

"Griff, maybe Phoenix would rather talk about something else a little less personal."

The kid looked understandably confused when he looked at his mom.

"The guy's sitting at our table after watching our drama when Bill stopped by. But me asking about his job is personal?"

Griff had a point. At this juncture, it was safe to say I had witnessed a very personal family moment. And both of them had a right to know who I was and who my father was, most especially Wren. She trusted me to spend time with Griffin. I should've already told her but it had been so fucking nice just being me for once—judged on *my* merit, not on a fucked-up family legacy.

"No, my father was not a cop," I started, then had to stop to swallow down the bile that had made its way up my throat. "He was a criminal."

"Criminal?" Griff's tone matched the unspoken shock on his mother's face. "What kind of criminal?"

Truth time.

My eyes went to Griff and not for the first time I wondered what his father looked like. The kid was all Wren.

He had her coloring, her height, her brown hair, her features, and the same blue eyes. I vaguely wondered if he knew how lucky he was that he bore no obvious resemblance to his father. In a cruel twist, I looked the most like Lester. Shiloh got more of our mother; she was near identical to her. My brothers and I got our height from Lester's side of the family. Echo towered over him, River a little taller, but I came eye to eye with the piece of shit, ever since I was thirteen. That was when he could no longer use his fists on me to express his displeasure. But he never did learn to keep his shitty comments to himself.

"When I was a kid, he stole cars," I told Griff. "By the time I was a teenager, he had a chop shop. When I was almost seventeen, he got arrested for murder."

Wren gasped, but Griff sucked in a breath so deep I could swear I felt the air whistle by my neck. Then I watched as a teenage boy wrestled with keeping his emotions in check—every blink, every twitch, every tremor that rocked through him.

"No way to cushion that for you, Griff," I explained.

"Murder?" The question whooshed out of his lungs and he lost all the bravado only a fourteen-year-old coming into his own could possess. He sounded like a little boy.

"Serving life for killing a cop," I finished the story.

"A cop?" Wren whispered and I didn't miss the disgust.

The repulsed look would come next, it always did. I'd seen it so many times I'd become immune. But I wasn't sure I could bear it coming from her. When I was a kid and people saw the Kent siblings their eyes slid away. There was no going to friends' houses or them coming to ours. There were no invites to birthday parties. There sure as fuck weren't birthday celebrations in our house when I was growing up. No one wanted their kids to associate with the

Kent siblings. And no one gave a shit what we were going through or what we had to live with, and no one cared to know we were nothing like our father—Echo made damn sure of that. He led us down a righteous path to atone for sins that were not ours. And here I was eighteen years later —a productive member of society, a good guy, a cop—and I still couldn't wash away the stench of the man who fathered me.

"Phoenix?" Wren's soft call brought me back to the room.

"Yes. My father's a cop killer."

Cop killer.

How many times had I heard people call Lester that? But had I ever uttered the phrase? I'm sure I had, but like everything else ugly in my life I probably blocked it out. How long would it take to blank this conversation? The sound of Wren's shock, the hurt I'd cause Griff, the vile truth.

The real question was how much more of my life was I going to sanitize? All the moments of discomfort I locked away so I didn't have to feel them. All those moments stole years of my life because I was still too much of a coward to face who I was and where I came from. It was easier to cleanse myself of the thoughts than unpack the boxes of emotional baggage I didn't want to deal with.

"So, you know," Griff murmured.

"I know," I confirmed.

"And you still left me." The hardness had crept back into his tone.

Fuck.

"I told you why—"

"That's bullshit!" he exploded.

Two chairs scraped against the wood floor— Griff's as he stood and Wren's as she jerked straight.

"Griff—"

Wren got no more out as Griff spoke over his mother, "You know what it's like. You know what people say. You *know*. You're the only one who does, and you left me because you thought I needed time? You think the stupid fire…" he trailed off and shook his head. "You know what, never mind. It doesn't matter. I don't need you."

With that lie still fresh in the air he stomped off in the direction of his room.

He'd punched the oxygen right out of my lungs and left me unable to reply.

"I need to go talk to him," Wren said as she pushed out of her chair.

She was wrong, *I* needed to be the one to talk to him, but I didn't correct her. I waited for her to disappear down the hall and like the fucking coward I was, I used their absence to escape.

I took my plate to the kitchen, scraped my uneaten meal into the trash, rinsed my plate, and loaded it into the dishwasher. After that, I booked it to the door and left before Wren came back and I had to face her judgment.

Once I was in my truck, I called the only person who could calm my thoughts.

It took three rings, but he answered. He always did.

"What's up, little brother?"

"Where you at?"

Echo paused. The cheerful tone of his voice was replaced with concern when he asked, "Where do you need me to be?"

Fucking Echo. Always the big brother. Always the protector, the shield, the one who gave up everything to take on his siblings and give us good.

I was not only a coward, I was also an asshole. A thirty-five-year-old man who was still calling his big brother for help after that brother had already given too much.

"I shouldn't've—"

"Where are you?" he interrupted me, and I knew I'd made a mistake.

Echo wouldn't give up. He was worse than a dog with a bone—more like a tiger in pursuit of a buffalo. He'd circle and run you around until you were too exhausted to fight him.

I seriously shouldn't've called him.

"Phoenix," he snapped impatiently.

"On my way home."

"How long?"

"Ten minutes."

"Meet you there."

Of course, he would. That was what Echo did; he dropped everything for me, River, and Shiloh. Without question, without hesitation, without a complaint. Since as far back as I could remember, Echo took care of our family. Even before Lester went away. If I allowed myself to think about it, I could remember the day our mom left. Lester went ballistic. He'd ranted for hours and fucking hours. The strangest part was the asshole seemed genuinely shocked the wife he called names, pushed around, and generally mistreated had taken off. Echo wasn't surprised. He slid into the role of caregiver, and he never stopped. The day our mom took off was the day he became a parent—he'd been Griffin's age taking care of three children.

Jesus.

Unfortunately, I spent the ten-minute drive thinking about Griffin. So when I got to my building and parked, my head was just as fucked-up as it was when I left Wren's. Further, by the time I walked into my apartment and found my brother sitting on my couch I hadn't been able to shove the memories back where they belonged.

I closed the door behind me and without preamble, I launched right in. "I fucked up and I don't know how to fix it. And now I'm not sure I should try."

Echo blinked at my blunt admission. Then he lounged back and waited for me to say more. When I didn't, he prompted, "Need more than that."

"You remember Griffin? The boy from the Hope Center?"

"I remember him *and* his mom."

Wren was sexy as fuck and only part of that had to do with her gorgeous face, pretty eyes, great ass, and long legs. So if anyone else had emphasized the "and" part of that statement I would've been murderous. But since it was Echo I was only mildly pissed.

"Right," I bit out.

Echo's gaze sharpened, going from brotherly concern straight to Lieutenant Kent.

"Maybe you wanna explain why you look like you're ready to rip my head off. And while you're at it, explain how you fucked up. We'll get to the fixing it part when I fully understand the scope of your stupidity."

No, I didn't want to explain why I was pissed that my brother had mentioned Wren even though I knew he meant nothing by it. Explaining how I'd been a royal asshole was easier. So that was what I did. I stood in my clean living room and told Echo everything. Some of it he knew because he'd volunteered at the Hope Center as well and had seen me with Griff. I skimmed over the parts that involved the fire because he was there for that, too, but also because he was my brother and I'd been trapped in a burning building —not his favorite topic. By the time I was done with my story the tables had turned and Echo looked like he wanted to rip my head off.

"You're shitting me," he growled.

Unfortunately, I wasn't. But I was unclear about which specific part he was referring to. Also, unfortunately, he went on to clarify.

"You're telling me after you spent weeks trying to earn that kid's trust you fucking *abandon* him?"

"I didn't abandon him," I defended. "I told you I was giving him time. You know what it's like with a victim; you're first on the scene, and it's you who is associated with the trauma. I didn't want to be a reminder. I wanted to give Wren and Griff some time to heal before—"

"Bullshit," he snapped. "Griffin wasn't a victim of a violent crime. Neither was Wren. But if we're being technical here, all three of you were victims of a traumatic event. And victims of a tragedy tend to find comfort *in each other*."

I wasn't a victim.

"I was giving them time."

"Again, bullshit."

Now I was getting angry.

"What the fuck does that mean?"

"It means that you were getting too close. I know about his dad, Phoenix. You see yourself in that kid and it's bringing up shit for you that you don't want to remember. But instead of coming to me, which, brother, I've been waiting decades for you to *come to me*, you break hard left and leave the kid hanging out there. The second part of that is Wren."

Since I wasn't going to acknowledge the first part of Echo's tirade, I focused on something else.

"What about Wren?"

Like a ten-year-old girl in the middle of a hissy fit, Echo rolled his eyes.

"I've seen her," he stated unhelpfully.

"I know you have."

"No, Phoenix, I've seen her with her boy. I've watched her watching you and her boy. I was there when you carried Griff out of that fire. I've also watched you watching her."

"So?"

"Christ," he ground out. "What's stopping you? You're into her and before you deny it, remember you're talking to the man who wiped your ass and your snotty nose."

I felt my lips curl into a grimace.

"You never wiped my ass."

"Jesus, Phoenix, what's stopping you?"

"Nothing."

"What the fuck is stopping you?"

"She has a kid!" I shouted.

Echo jerked back and disappointment suffused his face.

"Come again?"

"She's got a kid," I repeated. "I'm not a total dick. She's a single mother and I got no business fucking around with her when I have no intentions of taking us someplace meaningful."

"Because she has a kid?"

"Yes, because she has a kid, and I got no business being around a kid."

Lightning quick, Echo was off the couch and standing in front of me with his arms crossed. It sucked that at our age, I was still looking up at my big brother.

"Seems like being around him wasn't a problem when the two of you were playing ball at the Hope Center."

Fucking hell, what part of this was Echo not understanding?

"There's a difference and you damn well know it."

"No, brother, I don't know. Explain it to me," he demanded.

"Wren doesn't need me in her life fucking shit up when she's already got enough going on. And I'm not fit to raise a child."

My brother reared back like I'd landed a blow.

"Why the fuck aren't you fit to raise a child?"

"Seriously?" I snarled. "How the hell can you ask that? I got nothing to give. I don't have the first clue how to be a father, the man who raised me was a piece of shit—"

"*I* raised you!" Echo bellowed. "Me! I fucking raised you, not that asshole."

Fuck.

Acid burned in my gut worse than back at Wren's when Griff stormed off.

"Echo—"

"You think I had the first clue? You think I knew what the fuck I was doing? Clue in, Phoenix, no one does. Mom left, Dad was Dad and my choices were either leave you, River, and Shiloh to swing or pull my shit together and figure it out."

He sidestepped my coffee table and started for the door. When he got there, he stopped and faced me.

"Fix it. If not for you, for Griffin. But I hope you wake the fuck up and fix it not only for a kid who is walking the same path you've walked but for you, too. It's time you face the past. I know it was different for you than it was for me and River. Lester used you to manipulate the rest of us. But he also loved you and there's nothing wrong with that. You had something with him that the rest of us didn't and there's nothing wrong with that either—but it makes the betrayal worse for you. You had a father who paid attention to you, who showed you he cared, and it is okay to love that man but hate the murderer."

It was too hard to breathe.

The room was spinning, the walls were closing in, the air was thinning.

I couldn't fill my lungs.

Memories of my dad assaulted me. Taking me out to the garage with him. Smiling when I changed my first tire all by myself. His arm sliding around my shoulder as he told me how happy he was he had one son who was "*just like him.*"

"I don't love him," I whispered.

"Brother, you need to stop lying to yourself."

And with that Echo walked out, something he'd never done before—not before the problem was solved.

Until now.

Fix it. If not for you, for Griffin.

Fuck! I'd abandoned the kid. Not once, but twice.

5

You know those mornings where nothing goes right? Yeah, well, I was having one of those mornings after a night of tossing and turning, mulling over everything I should've said to Griff but didn't. Alternately, I was thinking about the things I had said that maybe I shouldn't have.

Then there was Phoenix.

After I'd had a brief conversation with my son, a conversation that was one-sided since he'd slid back into full-blown sulky teenager, I went back out into the kitchen to find Phoenix gone. At the time I wasn't sure if I was relieved or pissed. By the time I'd put away the leftovers and cleaned the kitchen, I thought I was relieved. But at some point, in the middle of the night as I tried to find a comfortable sleeping position, I'd switched to being angry.

After getting approximately two hours of sleep, I rolled out of bed and did my morning routine which weirdly did not include having to threaten bodily harm to the teen to get him out of bed. It did include my blow dryer sparking, filling my bathroom with the nauseating scent of burnt hair.

Not wanting to risk the rest of my hair going up in flames which would necessitate finding the time to shop for wigs, I opted for wet hair.

Total disaster.

I was not a wash-and-go kind of woman. Not because I was high maintenance but because my hair was neither curly nor straight. It was somewhere in the middle and not the sexy beachy waves that I envied. It was unruly which required blowing it out.

Then after dropping Griff off at school, I hit not one, but two accidents, making me almost forty-five minutes late for work. Thankfully, some of my coworkers had hit the same traffic. Not so thankfully I missed an important Zoom meeting.

Now I was sitting at my desk, grumpy, frazzled, drinking my first full cup of coffee, and staring at my phone reading a text message from Josie inviting me to lunch.

A boon.

An opportunity to have lunch with a woman who had her master's in early childhood development, a doctorate in education, and was the director of a boys and girls center —*yes, please*. Time and counsel I badly needed but wouldn't have reached out and asked for because I didn't want to be a burden.

I quickly tapped out my reply and got to work.

Ten minutes later, my assistant Vanessa was in my doorway, flush-faced and dreamy-eyed.

"Everything okay?" I smiled.

"Sorry to interrupt but there's an Officer Kent here to see you."

She breathed out the "Officer Kent" part of that statement.

"Phoenix is here?"

Vanessa's eyes rounded and a small smile tipped up her painted ruby-red lips.

"Of course his name is Phoenix. What other name would a man who looked like him have?"

I didn't answer mainly because I agreed. Phoenix's name fit and I'd thought that even before I watched him running out of a burning building through a wall of flames with my son cradled in his arms like he was a toddler and not a fourteen-year-old man-child who was nearly six feet tall.

Immortal.

"He doesn't have an appointment," Vanessa rightly pointed out. "Would you like me to tell him you're busy?"

Yes, *yes*, and yes, I wanted Vanessa to lie through her teeth and tell him I was buried under a mountain of work, and I wouldn't see my way through it until after the new year. I was not mentally prepared for another run-in with him two days in a row and three times in the last week.

Before I could put my thoughts in order Vanessa's grin turned into a full-blown smile. I recognized that smile—it was a man-eating smirk. She was my opposite in every way. Where I was tall, she was short, a pale blonde to my brunette, deep brown eyes to my blue, thin to my curves.

"Or," she purred. "I could invite him to coffee and you can duck out the back."

"You can send him in," I blurted out.

It was safe to say that in the short time I'd worked with her, she could read me. I was positive my face said everything I wasn't verbalizing. However, the thought of my very beautiful assistant having coffee with the very beautiful Phoenix made my stomach knot and unwarranted jealousy spike.

Some of her smile faded when she said, "You know I was joking, right?"

Was she? Did it matter? Phoenix Kent wasn't mine and never would be. He was simply a gorgeous man I thought way too much about to an unhealthy degree. A natural assumption would be hero worship. But seeing as my fantasies about him had started long before I watched him save my son's life, I'd concluded it wasn't gratitude that fueled my infatuation.

"It wouldn't matter if you weren't," I told her honestly.

"I don't have time to call bullshit. So I'll settle on you penciling me in for lunch this afternoon and you can fill me in on how you know Officer Kent."

I was grateful to inform her, "I have plans for lunch today."

"Lunch tomorrow then." Not a question. Vanessa would go back to her desk and block out an hour so she could pump me for information. "I'll send him back."

And with that, she bounced out of my office. Yes, bounced. Vanessa was thirty-two going on ten. If she wasn't so damn awesome, I'd hate her. Of course, that hate would stem from envy and since I didn't do catty it would last approximately five seconds.

Why have I never invited her over for dinner?

Maybe I'd been lost in my thoughts about why I'd kept my distance from Vanessa and everyone else I worked with when they were all great people. Or perhaps Phoenix's legs were so long due to his enormous size that it took him half the time it would take a normal person to walk down the hall to get to my office. Whatever the reason I was not ready for the sight of Phoenix Kent in full uniform. I'd seen him in his black cargos paired with a black t-shirt that clearly identified him as police, but I had not seen him totally geared up.

I could not stop my gaze from traveling the length of him

—from the mess of blond hair, down to the band of his black tee under a black-collared shirt which was under a black bulletproof vest. My eyes continued lower to the belt around his waist, to his holster, and handcuff pouch, down to his black cargo pants encasing his muscular thighs, his black boots, then back up to the shiny gold badge on his chest.

Good Lawd have mercy.

Two words: thirst trap.

"Wren?"

"Is that what you wear to get bad guys?" I insanely asked.

"Come again?"

"That vest doesn't even cover your stomach," I announced. "I mean, it does, but not down there." I pointed in the direction of his lower stomach just above his belt. "And shouldn't it go higher? What about your throat? You need a bigger vest."

When I was done with my ridiculous rant he smiled. Not just any old smile, a big, toothy smile that clearly stated he thought I was amusing.

"Can't sit in a vest if it covers my belt," he explained.

"Well, you're not sitting when you're catching bad guys," I pointed out.

"Kinda hard to run, too."

Okay, well, that made sense, too. But I still thought the police should have better body armor.

"But I do have a different vest when I go out with my unit."

I exhaled the breath I didn't realize I was holding. This was unfortunate seeing as the breath I released was audible—meaning Phoenix heard it, and when he did, his smile got bigger. That smile ratcheted up the sexy-man-in-uniform vibes that were filling my office, flowing over me, and settling in areas that hadn't seen male attention in so long I couldn't remember the last time they'd been touched.

Without my permission—or maybe subconsciously—my gaze dropped to the handcuff pouch on the left side of his belt. All sorts of wildly inappropriate fantasies filled my mind. Starting with the good old-fashioned cops and robbers roleplay to hightailing my ass to the nearest gas station to steal a pack of gum.

Yes, I was seriously considering committing a crime to get those handcuffs locked around my wrists.

"Wren?"

"Hm?"

"Babe." He chuckled and my eyes darted away from his belt to the bookshelf behind him.

Damn.

This wasn't working, I couldn't be in the same room with him without turning into a...a what? Sex-starved woman on the prowl? A floozy? A woman who was dangerously close to contemplating felonious acts to get laid.

"This isn't working," I bluntly told him.

"What isn't?"

"All of it."

Phoenix took another step into my office and dipped his head toward the chair in front of my desk.

"Mind if I sit?"

I minded a great deal. Though sitting meant I wasn't eye level with his crotch so maybe it was a good idea for him to sit. On the other hand, if he sat he'd be closer and I'd have a better view of his perfectly chiseled jaw. Not to mention those eyes. They were undeniably the most beautiful pair of eyes I'd seen outside of my son's.

"Actually, I have a lot of work..."

Phoenix moved around the chair and sat.

"How's Griff?"

That reminded me; I was pissed at him.

"He's not talking."

"Right. I came by to ask if I could pick him up after school today."

"I'm not sure—"

"You know that for me to volunteer at the Hope Center I had to pass a background check and I'm a cop," he needlessly pointed out.

I was so confused by his words that the change in him barely registered. But when it did, I was chilled to the bone. Sexy-man-in-uniform Phoenix had vanished. I stared at him sitting across from me and all hints of his beautiful smile were gone. He'd retreated safely behind his wall.

"What?"

"Figured you'd understand better than anyone."

"Understand what?"

Phoenix's eyes turned hard, and I felt mine narrow in return.

We were locked in a squinty-eyed stare down, neither of us saying anything. Then it dawned on me—he thought I was judging him for his father's crimes.

Oh. My. God.

My temper flared and before I thought better of it, I spoke.

"I cannot believe you'd think that," I hissed as I leaned forward. "You are no more responsible for what your father did than Griff is for Conor being who he is. And how dare you think I'm some sort of judgmental bitch."

Some of the harshness left his features, but since I was pissed at him for numerous reasons, I continued, "What the hell? This is about Griff needing some time."

"Wrong," he cut in before I could say more. "Made that mistake as he rightly pointed out last night."

"Yeah, about last night. You left."

I watched him flinch before he nodded.

"That was a mistake, too. I own it. I should've gone back and talked to him but straight up my head was fucked. It's not often I talk about my father and being around Griffin—knowing what he's dealing with, how he's feeling, seeing myself in him—I didn't know how to sort through my thoughts, so I left."

It was my turn to flinch, but mine was more like a jerk seeing as it felt like he'd thrust a dagger through my heart. In all my worry and all my selfish thoughts, I'd not considered what Phoenix was feeling after he'd talked about his father. My concern for Griff outweighed everything.

But beyond that, deep into the night when I became angry at Phoenix, I knew it was because he'd left me.

Always alone.

I'd walked into my house after work to find him cooking. He'd stood next to me during the drama with Bill. He'd sat at my table for dinner and through all of that I knew it wasn't real, but it had felt good.

Then he was gone, and that feeling was gone with him, and it hurt.

Damn.

"Phoenix—"

"He was right about something else, and I mean no offense but I'm the only one who knows what he's going through. Well, me, Echo, and River."

I hated when people said "no offense" when they knew they were going to strike a blow.

I ignored his insinuation I didn't understand what my son was going through when I damn well did.

I leaned forward and said, "What's interesting is you don't include your sister in that asshole remark."

Phoenix shifted in his chair and scooted forward, pinning me with an icy glare.

"I reckon on some level Shiloh gets it. But it's not the same. A boy who's growing into a young man looks to his father to show him the way. A young man who's coming into his own deciding on the man he's going to be looks to the man who fathered him either in hopes he lives up to all that man taught him or he wonders if he's got the same demons. Shiloh feels the loss of what girls learn from their fathers, and I'm not saying what a father teaches his girl is any less important, but it is different. The same as Shiloh feels our mother's abandonment differently than me and my brothers. She lost the woman who was supposed to show her the way. I'm not a woman, but I do know that what Shiloh lost me and my brothers could never give her, and we tried."

Holy shit.

The bricks and mortar that constructed his walls were becoming clear. The monumental life-changing events that could send big, tall, strong Phoenix Kent into hiding.

What had him so broken he thought he could never be fixed?

I grew up in a house with two parents bickering and fighting until they split up. Then the fighting just got uglier, only they did it from two separate houses. That meant it was never-ending for me.

"You're wrong. A girl looks to her father for the same. She looks to him for guidance. He's supposed to be the one to teach her how a man is supposed to love her. When he fails at that she looks elsewhere, and she searches blindly, which can lead to not good things."

Boy was that an understatement.

"Wren," he called gently.

"I'm sorry about your mom."

"It doesn't—"

I held my hand up, shook my head, and softly whispered, "Don't do that. There are special things a momma teaches her boy. Special things you didn't get. And for that, I am truly sorry."

Another silent stare down ensued, only this time it didn't come with narrowed eyes and irritation. His guard was down, and I hoped I was showing him the same.

It was reckless, both of us vulnerable and open.

This conversation had to end, not only because I was at work but because I needed to protect myself from any more complications.

"I have to get back to work," I told him.

"Right. About Griff, I'd like to get him from school. We can go back to my place and hang until you're done with work, then I'll bring him home."

Griff would not be happy about that. But Phoenix was right, he did understand, and if there was a chance—even the tiny, tiniest one he could get Griff to open up—then I was willing to try.

"One condition. Actually two."

He jerked his chin which I took as macho-speak for continue.

"The first is you have to promise me his homework will get done. And the second is that your head is where it needs to be, and you won't disappear on my son."

Or disappear on me.

I obviously didn't say that out loud. But I was thinking it and that was a red flag.

"Homework. Saddling me with the heavy lifting," he joked.

He wasn't wrong but still, I pointed out, "I'm being serious."

"My head's straight and I'm not going anywhere."

God, I hope he's telling the truth.

"Okay. I'll text Griff and tell him."

"You gotta get back to work," he reminded me. "I'll text him, that way when he texts back his reply it'll be me who deals with it."

That was Phoenix's nice way of telling me when Griff texted back a shitty teenage reply which was sure to happen, he'd take the hit.

As if to punctuate the end of our discussion my office phone rang, and Phoenix stood.

"I'll let you get that. I'll text you after I pick up Griff."

I was mesmerized by his ass in his cargos, so engrossed in my internal debate about which was better—watching him walk in or walk out—I didn't get a chance to thank him before he was gone.

I picked up my phone and got to work.

An hour later Josie texted me back to set up lunch, which she ended up having to schedule for the next day. Before I set down my phone, I made a decision and sent a message to Vanessa to ask if she was free that afternoon.

My phone chimed immediately with her one-word reply: *Absolutely*.

I gave myself a moment to ponder why I hadn't reached out and tried to make friends before now, then I decided it didn't matter.

I was moving on.

∽

My BLT was halfway to my mouth when Vanessa's eyes widened.

"Do you believe in kismet?" she whispered.

This felt like a trick question. Or maybe more like a no-right-answer question. What if she believed in fate and was about to tell me it was kismet, I'd landed in Georgia so we could be BFFs?

Thankfully, she didn't wait for me to answer before she jerked her head toward the line of people waiting in front of the coffee counter with her eyes still comically bulging.

"You see that guy?"

Not wanting to be obvious that I was looking in case 'that guy' was looking in our direction I moved only my eyeballs to the counter.

"I see three guys," I quietly returned.

Apparently, Vanessa didn't care about obvious when she pointed her finger at one of the guys.

"Him. The one in that black t-shirt."

"Stop pointing before he sees you."

"Why would I care if he sees me? That's the point."

I slid my gaze back to the line and found the guy in the black shirt. Tall but not overly so, nice build, biceps that stretched the material of his tee, and messy brown hair. I couldn't see much else since I only had his side profile in view. But from what I could see he was good looking.

"Yeah, I see him."

"So, do you believe in kismet?"

Oh, no, what if I said yes and that prompted her to run over to this man, jump into his arms, and profess her undying love?

Why was making new friends so hard?

No, why did *I* make it so hard?

"Um...no, not really."

Vanessa looked back at the guy and shook her head, but she did it smiling.

When she looked back over at me, she picked up her bottle of water and muttered, "Yeah, neither do I."

I couldn't keep from glancing back at the line. The guy in the black shirt hadn't moved, but he was now looking at Vanessa.

"Do you know him?"

"No, but I keep running into him."

Red flags started waving.

"Running into him like he's stalking you?"

For some strange reason, this made Vanessa bust out laughing. I didn't see the humor; she was beautiful and the world was a scary place these days.

I did another check of the line and found the guy still staring. This time he was smiling.

Wow.

Okay, he was good looking but when he smiled he was hot.

I really hope I don't think a crazy stalker is hot.

"Not like that." Vanessa shook her head for added emphasis. "A few weeks ago I saw him at Balls Deep—"

"Where?" I sputtered.

"It's a pool hall." Her explanation was accompanied by a chuckle. "It used to be called just Balls, wait, the name wasn't *Just* Balls, it was Balls without the deep after the balls." I couldn't help but laugh at Vanessa's animated commentary. "Someone bought it and renamed it Balls Deep. It used to be a total dive, now it's a hot spot. So, anyway I was there with some friends and so was he. Then I saw him in the grocery store. He was reading the back of a peanut butter jar and didn't even look up. Next, I saw him at the gas station. He was putting the nozzle back into the pump when I pulled in on the other side. Yesterday I saw him at the gym when I was leaving. And now he's here."

"That's why you asked if I believe in kismet because you keep seeing him?"

"Yep. I've never seen him before but in the last two weeks I've seen him five times."

I wasn't sure I believed in kismet but I did think that people were meant to come in and out of your life for a reason. Different lessons needed to be learned. Wisdom needed to be shared. Compassion needed to be spread. The hardest part for me had always been accepting that not every person who crossed my path was meant to stay for a lifetime. It was the out part that hurt, and that was why I needed to keep a good amount of distance between me and Phoenix. "So, why did it take this long for us to do lunch?"

Shit.

Friending is so freaking hard.

"I'm not anti-social," I defended. "I just have a hard time with new people. I'm not boring or anything. I like having fun and all. I'm just, I don't know…"

"Like everyone else who isn't in elementary school? I mean, how come it was so easy to make friends when you still chewed with your mouth open and probably picked your nose and flicked the booger—okay, so the boys were the only ones doing that, but still. It was so easy then, but now why is meeting someone new and making friends so difficult? Is it because back then we didn't give two shits what people thought about us? Or is it because back then we weren't old enough to rack up regrets and baggage so really the only thing you were getting judged on was your clothes, shoes, hairstyle, and acne? By the way, I had really bad acne, glasses, and braces, so people were nasty little assholes to me."

Beautiful Vanessa had acne and people were assholes to her?

"Well, sister, I'd say you're now winning in a big way. You're freaking gorgeous. Not that being beautiful makes the person but if that's the yard stick you were being measured by in elementary school then I'd said you got those bitches by a mile."

"Right, says the woman who looks like Megan Fox only taller and hotter. And since we're on that topic let's talk about Officer Phoenix Kent." She stopped and waved her hand in front of her face. "Holy hell, that man is hot. If I wasn't afraid it would get me fired, I might admit I scrolled IG to check if he was on any Hot Cop accounts."

I wasn't sure I wanted to know the answer to that, but I asked anyway, "Was he?"

"Sadly, no."

The sound of a glass shattering made Vanessa and me glance at the door. Black t-shirt guy was kneeling in front of a woman picking up a broken mug. The woman in front of him was looking down and gawking at him.

Vanessa righted herself and muttered, "He's not that good-looking, sheesh."

I bit back a smile. Someone sounded awfully jealous.

"Have you thought maybe to stop and talk to him one of the times you've seen him?"

Those brown eyes of hers widened right before she scrunched her nose.

"What? No way. I don't approach men. And that's not because of some stupid notion men should make the first move or I'm up my own ass. I'm thirty-two and have learned that if a man wants my attention, he's gonna have to work for it. Period. I used to put myself out there but after being burned one too many times I learned. Not that I still don't get fucked, but it's just that they have to work harder before they screw me over."

"I totally get that. My ex-husband landed the *coup de grâce* of screw-overs."

"How'd he screw you over?"

I sucked in a breath and reminded myself Conor's crimes were not mine. I'd done nothing to be ashamed or embarrassed about.

"Hang tight, friend, it's a long story."

Vanessa sat back, grabbed her water, and smiled.

"Hit me with it."

So at her invitation, I hit her with it.

When I was done, we went back to work and she treated me no differently.

I was just Wren, not the ex-wife of a murderer.

6

The passenger door to my truck was wrenched open at the same time my cell phone rang. I ignored the phone in favor of the sulking teenager.

"Yo! What'd my truck do to you?"

"Nothin'," Griff mumbled. "Why are you here?"

Clearly, the kid wasn't over his snit. After our text exchange, I was actually surprised he got into my truck willingly.

The ringing continued. Griff looked at the display in my dash, then back to me and asked a new question, "Who's Chelsea?"

I didn't answer the kid but I did answer the call.

"Hello?"

"Phoenix," she angrily clipped.

"What's wrong?"

Without missing a beat my friend Matt's woman, Chelsea, launched in, "I'll tell you what's wrong, I'm gonna be arrested if—"

Fuck.

"Where are you?"

"An old farm outside of Hollow Point off one-ninety-six."

"Where's Matt?"

"In the middle of a class."

Matt Kessler worked at Triple Canopy with my sister Shiloh's fiancé, Luke. Not only did TC do security work they also did civilian and law enforcement tactical training. If Matt was in the middle of a class he wouldn't have his phone.

"Buckle up, bud."

I waited until he was buckling up then pulled away from the curb.

"I'm on my way but I need to know what I'm headed into."

"You'll see!"

"I've got Griffin with me—"

"Not you, I was talking to Milo."

"Who's Milo?"

Chelsea did not inform me who Milo was, nor did she explain to me what the hell was going on but she sure as shit had a foul mouth when she continued to shout at this Milo character.

I chanced a look at Griff. He was gawking at the screen in my dash. Wren would not have been happy.

Shit.

"Chels, I'm on my way. Before I hang up, are you in danger?"

"Me? No. But I'm gonna string up this motherfucker and whip him bloody if you don't hurry up."

Jesus.

"What's the name of the farm?"

"Can't miss it. Red split-rail fence. Big sign at the end of the lane says, Riggins." She paused, then, "I'm taking 'em, you asshole."

"I'll be there in ten."

I disconnected the call and immediately hit my brother's contact.

It rang three times before he answered, "Yeah?"

"I need backup. Where are you?"

"Leaving the station. Where are you?"

I quickly explained what was going on.

Echo didn't hesitate.

"On my way."

"Think you should call around and get word to Matt. I got Griff with me, need to talk to him before we get there."

"Copy."

Echo disconnected but before I could explain, Griff piped up, "You think she'd really whip him bloody?"

Yes.

I pushed down on the accelerator, yet not as hard as I wanted.

"No telling."

"Seriously?"

I thought about how to explain Chelsea.

"She's a bull rider."

"A bull rider?" he questioned. "Like in a rodeo?"

"Yep. She had to quit after this last season."

I checked my mirror, changed lanes, and sped up.

"Why'd she quit?"

"She got hurt."

"Like a bull stomped her?"

"Not stomped but she got bucked off, broke her ribs and her shoulder. She went through PT and rehab and went back to training. Rode in another rodeo and had to make a choice to continue on and risk permanent injury or give it up and let her body heal."

"Was she good?"

"Hell yeah. I've got a video of her last ride on my phone. I'll show you later."

"Cool."

Wait. What?

Cool?

That was it.

The kid was giving me whiplash.

As if I'd cursed my luck, Griff's attitude made a swift U-turn and came back full force.

"Why'd you pick me up?"

He didn't ask out of curiosity; his tone was full of accusation, and once again I found myself backed into a very uncomfortable corner.

A corner I was not ready to discuss in my truck heading into an unknown situation. One that was potentially dangerous. Also, one that Wren would likely have my balls for taking her kid to.

"Listen, when we get to the farm, I want you to stay in the truck with the doors locked."

"What? Why?"

My phone ringing meant I didn't answer his ridiculous question.

"Shiloh?"

"Echo called, I'm on my way."

"Did you get a hold of Luke?"

"Yeah, he's going to get Matt now but Matt's out on the rifle range."

Shit.

"Listen, I have Griffin with me—"

"Echo told me. I'm on shift, ran into Ethan, told him

what's going on, and he's lights and sirens. He should be there before you."

That was doubtful. I was coming up on my exit.

"I don't need a babysitter," Griff grouched from beside me.

Jesus.

"See you when you get there," I told Shiloh and disconnected.

"Alright, Griff, here's the deal. We're headed into a situation that is likely dangerous. You heard Chelsea, she's pissed off. I've known Chelsea for a while and I've never heard her lose her cool like that. I don't know why she's there or who's there with her and that makes me nervous. In a situation like this, anything can happen. Telling my brother and sister I have you is not about you needing a babysitter, it's about keeping you safe. They know that if the shit hits the fan or something happens to me, I want you protected."

"You want me protected?"

"Of course I want you protected."

"Because if I get hurt my mom will be mad at you?"

Damn, but I'd fucked up royally.

"No, Griff, because I don't want anything to happen to you."

"Why'd you pick me up?"

This kid came in second place after Echo in the wear-you-down by repetitive questioning.

"I told you why."

"But last night you left."

Last night, I left *again*.

"Last night was intense. You and your mom had a lot going on. She needed to talk to you—"

"You keep saying that and leaving then coming back."

Nothing like being called out by a teenager.

"Okay, Griff, we don't have time to get into this right now, but I'm gonna remind you that *you* keep telling me you don't want me around. You got up from the table and went to your room. If you had something to say to me then you should've stayed and said your piece."

I saw the red split-rail fence coming up and off in the distance was a huge barn that had seen better days.

"There's the fence." Griff pointed to the farm.

What he didn't have was a comeback.

"I think my mom's mad at me about reading the letters my dad sent."

"Yeah? Did she tell you that?" I asked as I pulled onto the long gravel lane.

A plain ranch-style home was set back to the left. No landscaping around the house but there were acres of neatly kept grass.

"No, but she was hiding them in her nightstand, and I took them, so I know she's mad."

"Not cool snoopin' in your mom's stuff."

The gravel road curved to the left and opened up to barns. Chelsea's old, rusty pickup with her horse trailer attached was parked next to a fenced-in paddock. Three gangly-looking horses were gathered around a pile of what looked like hay.

And then it became clear.

Why Chelsea was on the warpath.

Horses.

I scanned the area and there was no Chelsea or this Milo guy who I assumed was the rancher who owned the horses.

"When I get out, doors locked," I reminded him. "And if you hear or see something you don't like, do not get out, call nine-one-one."

"I thought your brother and sister were coming. They're police, right?"

"Yeah, but I still want you calling emergency."

"Okay, yeah, I'll call nine-one-one."

When I got close to Chelsea's truck, I parked, left the truck running, and looked over at Griffin.

"You know how to drive?"

His eyes practically bugged out of his head when he mumbled, "Um. I'm fourteen."

Right. Fourteen. Sometimes I forgot it wasn't normal for a father to teach his ten-year-old how to drive like mine did. Looking back, I was fairly certain my dad had taught me in hopes he could send me out to nab cars.

I turned off the ignition and kept Griff's attention.

"Do not get out."

"Jeez. I heard you. I won't get out."

"Be right back."

I jumped out of my truck and looked around the yard noting the general state of disrepair that was in stark contrast to the house and the front lawn. From the highway, you'd never know that the back looked like a junkyard, and it smelled worse. Not the normal smells of a working farm. The air reeked of rot and horse shit.

I heard raised voices and took off in the direction of the barn praying that rot wasn't dead animals.

I heard Chelsea shout, "Over my dead body!"

Next came, "Don't fuckin' tempt me."

That was when I went from a jog to an all-out sprint.

I hit the barn, ran through the open door, and found Chelsea with her back to an older man who was holding a shotgun. With no fucks given that she had a gun pointed at her back, Chelsea was tending to a horse that looked like it was half the weight it should've been. Even from a distance,

I could see the ridge of its backbone and deep indents around its ribs.

"Step back," I demanded.

The old-as-dirt man who I assumed was Milo swung the shotgun in my direction. My hand automatically went to my hip but came up empty.

Fuck.

"Git!" he yelled. "You're trespassin'."

Chelsea ignored Milo and the gun and looked over at me. The anger I thought I'd see was absent. She looked the picture of devastation mixed with terror and I knew it had nothing to do with being held at gunpoint.

"Put the gun down and step away from Chelsea."

"She's tryin' to steal my horse. I have a right to protect my property."

Christ.

"I'm not stealing anything, you jackass. I'm saving them."

Them?

Oh, shit, she was planning on taking more than one.

The sound of sirens wailed in the distance, and I hoped Ethan got there before I had to tackle a ninety-year-old man.

"I'm a police—"

Milo cut me off to demand, "I want her arrested."

"Alright. Put the gun down and we'll talk," I told him and walked closer.

The man might've been close to kicking the bucket, but I didn't stand a chance against the shotgun he had pointed at me.

"Put the gun down!" I heard Echo shout from behind me.

Milo did not put the gun down. He swung it wildly while yelling, "I want her arrested."

"Sure thing, after you put the gun down," Echo lied.

I glanced back at Chelsea who was completely disregarding what was happening around her. She focused all of her attention on the emaciated horse in front of her. The horse rested its jaw on her shoulder, and if I didn't know any better, I'd think she was the only thing keeping the poor beast on its feet. Then again, considering the state of the animal, she might've been.

I took in the rest of the barn.

Fury ignited.

There was no extinguishing this kind of anger. The kind that came from deep within, the kind that would burn straight through, the kind that any decent human would feel and would never forget.

Cruelty beyond comprehension.

"When was the last time that horse ate?" I asked.

"None of—"

"When the fuck was the last time that horse ate?" I asked again.

That shotgun leveled on me, and I was done.

In a moment of pure stupidity, I rushed Milo.

"Phoenix."

At my brother's warning, I changed my course of action. Instead of tackling the old man which likely would've led to more damage than was necessary, I grabbed the barrel of the shotgun, and with one quick jerk, I yanked it out of his grasp. Though I thought the asshole deserved whatever damage I could inflict seeing as he'd grossly mistreated his animals. Not to mention he'd pointed a gun at Chelsea. He was lucky Echo and I were here first. If Matt had shown up before us and found his woman at gunpoint, Milo would've already been put down.

Milo stumbled, pitched to the side, and barely caught

himself on a lawn tractor. Unfortunately, this meant he kept his feet when he opened his mouth.

"I want you all arrested."

Jesus.

"Shut up, Milo, and move outta the way," Chelsea instructed.

"You're not—"

"I am," she broke in. "I'm taking all of them and you're gonna let me or I'm calling in animal control."

That begged the question of why she hadn't done that in the first place instead of coming out here alone.

When Milo made no effort to step aside, she stepped away from the horse, whirled around, and advanced so quickly I couldn't stop her before she was in the old man's space. So I did the only thing I could do without physically removing her—I took her back.

"How dare you," she hissed. "How fucking dare you treat these animals this way, you heartless piece of shit. How long has she been locked in that stall? When was the last time you gave her grain or fresh water?"

"Fuck you, Chelsea, she's aggressive—"

"Yeah, is she? I would be, too, if you tried to starve me to death. But she's not aggressive now, is she? No, she's damn near dead."

Milo lifted his arm but before he could carry out whatever act of lunacy he was planning I grabbed his wrist.

"Don't," I warned.

"What the fuck is going on?" Matt roared.

Chelsea jolted. Her hand went up in a conciliatory gesture that was in no way going to calm my friend down as he stalked farther into the fray.

She had to know it was pointless, but she still asked, "Please don't yell."

"Please don't yell?" he returned. "I pull behind your Ram *and* trailer. First thing I see is three horses going at a pile of hay like they hadn't eaten in a week. Then I get a good look at them, and I figure I was wrong, it hadn't been a week, more like a month. Then the fucking stench hits me before I walked into the filthiest fucking barn I've ever seen and find this fucker in your face and you're asking me not to yell?"

Matt's gaze went from Chelsea to the open stall behind her, and I knew the moment he saw it. His face went from hard and angry to rightfully murderous.

"Echo," I called out, but my brother was already on the move.

"What. The. Fuck?" Matt growled.

My brother's hand curled around Matt's shoulder, halting his progress.

"Holy shit," Ethan grumbled as he joined us. His head swiveled, taking in the mess before he pinned Milo with a scathing look. "Are you the owner of this farm?"

With Echo, Ethan, and Matt there that meant they could handle this situation. If I had to hear Milo say he wanted Chelsea arrested one more time I was going to lose my ever-loving mind.

"I need to go check on Griff," I announced.

Matt's gaze came to me, then dropped to the shotgun still in my hand and he asked, "Whose is that?"

Fuck.

"Matt..." Chels started but trailed off when her fiancé shook his head.

"We'll talk about that when I get back," I told him.

"Please tell me that motherfucker wasn't in possession of that when you got here."

The level of Matt's self-control was damn impressive. If

I'd walked in and some asshole was up in Wren's face, I would've lost my shit.

Wait.

What?

Why the hell did my mind go straight to Wren?

I quickly blinked away that thought and decided it was best I not answer Matt before Ethan had Milo safely in cuffs. I figured if given the opportunity Matt would do more than tackle the old man when he found out the barrel of the shotgun had been inches from Chelsea's back.

"I gotta check on Griff," I reiterated and watched Matt squint.

He was not stupid, not by a long shot. He knew exactly whose gun I was holding, and he knew it had been pointed at Chelsea.

The cop in me had the urge to protect Milo from a beating and Matt from an assault charge. The human in me couldn't summon up the desire to help a man who would treat an animal so poorly. If Matt's control slipped, I didn't think a man in that barn would've moved to stop him, and Chelsea sure as shit wouldn't stop her man.

Those were my pointless thoughts as I walked out of the barn. Pointless because I knew the former SEAL wouldn't slip. Pointless because as much as Ethan would turn a blind eye for a moment or two, a good man taught him to be honorable in a way that wouldn't allow him to cross the lines that Echo and I would.

As soon as I rounded the corner, I saw the passenger side door of my truck open, and my heart rate spiked.

Where the hell was Griffin?

7

Movement by Chelsea's trailer caught my attention and I saw the back of Griff as he ran toward the fence. Next, I saw my sister chasing after him.

Shit.

And for the second time that afternoon I took off in a sprint to catch up with the pair, but I came to an abrupt stop when they came into view along with Luke and Dylan. I should've known Matt wouldn't have come alone and off the job. Luke would never allow my sister to go into an unknown situation without him taking her back. The man took protective to a whole new level, one of the many reasons I welcomed him into the family when he and Shiloh got engaged. As far as I was concerned there was no better man for my baby sister.

"Griff, stay by the fence," Dylan instructed as he slowly approached one of the horses.

"Do you think you can catch him?" Griff asked and there was no missing the hopefulness in his tone.

The horse didn't move when Dylan attached a rope to his bridle.

Well, that answered that question, though if the beast was fighting fit, I found it doubtful Dylan would've had such an easy time of it.

"You want me to open it yet?" Griff was already unlatching the chain.

I wasn't sure how I felt about Wren's son participating in felony theft. However, I was positive Wren would be sure how she felt, and I knew that feeling would be extreme anger at me for allowing it.

"Yeah, bud, but stay on the other side." Dylan slowly led the weak horse toward the fence. Each step the animal took looked painful.

Griff stayed behind the gate as he swung it open for Dylan while Shiloh and Luke tried to catch the other two horses in the pasture.

When the gate was fully open, I caught sight of Griff's face and suddenly I had no doubts about his involvement. No trace of the angry teenager. No sign of the indignant kid. No flicker of the hurt he tried to conceal. Nothing but empathy registered.

Wren might be pissed but her wrath was a small price to pay to witness a young man's compassion.

Dylan and the horse cleared the gate. Griff started to close it but froze when he saw me. I watched as his shoulders tensed thinking I was going to be mad that he didn't listen. Maybe I should've been. Maybe a father would've known what to do, but since I wasn't one, I went with my gut.

"You good out here with Shiloh and the guys?" I asked.

Stark relief showed on his face when he answered, "Yeah."

I glanced back into the pasture to find Luke staring at me. With a lift of his chin, he silently told me he'd keep an eye on Griff. I dipped mine in return and my gaze slid to my sister. She gave me a small, sad smile.

I returned that as well and headed back to the barn.

By the time I made it back inside, Ethan had Milo in cuffs. Matt and Echo were helping Chelsea guide the skinniest horse I'd ever seen out of the stall. The animal was so weak it would be a miracle if they were able to load it into the trailer.

"Liar!" Milo yelled. "You told me you'd arrest her."

Was he fucking insane?

"I never told you that. And how you thought you weren't going to be the one leaving here in cuffs I don't understand."

"They're mine! I—"

"They *were* yours, asshole. Now they are not."

Ethan gave Milo a gentle shove to get him moving. I had to hand it to the man—he was far gentler than I would've been and in hindsight, I should've tackled the motherfucker.

"If she takes my horses, I'll—"

Before Matt could get to Milo, I stepped between the two men and leaned down so all he could see was my face.

"I wouldn't finish that threat in front of three cops," I advised.

A look I didn't like flared in the old man's eyes. A look I'd seen a lot over the years when I'd made an arrest. Not the understanding that he was well and truly fucked, not awareness that the inside of a jail cell was imminent, not remorse for the crimes committed. The flashing of blame was what worried me. The flashing of an accusation like it was somehow Chelsea's fault he was a dick, or Ethan's, or mine for that matter. Normally when my team made an arrest, we were protected by anonymity—our faces were covered, we were gloved, and the rest of our kit hid any tattoos. I got to go home from a takedown and not worry that some asshole was going to follow me home. And there were safeguards put in place when we needed to testify. But right then I was exposed and I sure as fuck didn't like that Chelsea was vulnerable.

Proving he was more than the piece of shit I already knew him to be, Milo didn't heed my warning and added stupidity.

"When a man's home has been violated and his property stolen it's not a threat when he says there will be hell to pay."

I'd agree with that if the property he was referring to wasn't animals that had been so badly neglected one of them was knocking on death's door and the others weren't far behind.

"Let's go," Ethan ordered and used Milo's cuffed hands to propel him forward. "I'm taking him in, check in later."

"Will do."

Ethan was almost to the door when I called out to stop him. "Careful taking him out front."

Understanding I didn't want Milo to see my sister and Griffin, he jerked his chin.

"Copy that."

"Chelsea, baby—" Matt started, then abruptly stopped and sighed.

"Don't." Chelsea's painful plea had the hard edges around my heart cracking. "Just don't say it. I have to try. She deserves a chance and I'm giving it to her."

"Alright, let's get her to the trailer."

It was a long, slow, arduous process getting the horse out of the barn. It was even more complicated getting her into the trailer. But the relief on Chelsea's face once all the horses were loaded made it worth it. Knowing that four beautiful creatures were going to get the love and care they deserved meant everything.

Griff and I stood next to my truck and watched Chelsea drive away. Then we stood there longer while Matt, Luke, Dylan, Shiloh, and Echo got into the vehicles.

Once Dylan backed his Jeep up, I turned to Griff to tell him to get in, but the words died in my throat and my chest compressed with the struggle I saw on the kid's face.

Fucking shit.

I never should've left him to help Shiloh and the others. I should've known fucking better. The kid was fourteen.

"Hey," I called.

Without looking at me Griffin turned and gave me his back.

Goddamn it.

"Need you to talk to me, bud."

Griff shook his head, and I heard him sniff.

Goddamn fuck.

I put my hand on his shoulder and the moment I did he attempted to shrug it off. My fingers curled around, careful not to scare him but with enough force to know I wasn't letting go. I debated if it was the right move; touching him in general seemed like a boundary I shouldn't cross, touching him when he clearly didn't want me to more so, but this was way too fucking critical.

"Listen up, Griffin, this is important." I gave his shoulder a quick squeeze. "A man, a real man does not hide his emotions. If you think that today, what we all saw, didn't gut every single one of us you are wrong. Men, real men show kindness and compassion. I saw you, Griff, I saw you watching those animals limp out of that field and I know you felt it. I saw it. So don't hide that now."

Griff shrugged again and this time I let my hand fall away. Slowly he craned his neck to look back at me. The agony etched in his features made me feel like the worst kind of person. He was too young to see what he saw.

"Did you see..." Griff trailed off and I watched his chin wobble.

"I saw," I confirmed even though I wasn't entirely sure what he was referring to.

But the scene as a whole was bad enough, I didn't need to see a particular detail to understand the situation was fucked up.

"That last one..."

Again he didn't finish and again I didn't need him to.

Tears were brimming and I knew he was trying his best to suck it up and stop them from falling.

"You had to...it couldn't walk up the ramp. You guys picked it up."

"We did."

"Why would someone do that?"

Fuck.

The tears rolled down his cheeks.

"I can't answer that, son. I can't comprehend how someone could be so cruel. I don't *want* to understand."

Griff's hand lifted and he angrily swiped the tears away.

"You probably think I'm weak—"

"There's not a goddamn thing weak about giving those animals your tears. Hear this, Griffin, a man isn't the sort of man I want to know if what we saw today doesn't rock him to his core. You being man enough to give those animals what you've giving them right now is a beautiful thing." I stopped long enough to draw in a breath. "Men cry. And anyone who tells you otherwise is a goddamn liar."

Griff startled back in surprise.

"Before we leave, I need to know you get me."

"I get you," he murmured softly.

Thank fuck.

"I want you to take me to the vet clinic."

"Griff—"

"I want to go, Phoenix."

Jesus Christ, I was not cut out to be in charge of a teenage boy. At that point, I would've done anything to make the pain in his eyes disappear.

Goddamn anything.

"Sure. We can go."

There was a beat of silence while Griff swallowed and closed his eyes so tightly, they wrinkled.

"I don't understand," he told me. "And I'm like you, I don't want to. I don't ever want to understand how someone can hurt someone like that."

Jesus. Was he talking about Milo and the horses or about his father killing someone?

8

To say I was confused would be a gross understatement.

After a crazy day at work, which included lunch with Vanessa, I was exhausted, and my eyes were blurry from staring at a computer screen for hours proofreading grant proposals. All I wanted to do was go home and do something I never did—open a bottle of wine and drink my dinner. Instead, I'd driven across town to pick up Griff from a man named Matt Kessler's house. After I arrived, I realized I'd seen him at the Hope Center a few times along with his fiancée Chelsea. But they weren't alone. Phoenix's sister Shiloh and her fiancé Luke, Dylan Welsh and his fiancée Sawyer—whom I'd met once were also there.

Within two minutes of my arrival, my son launched into a story that had my head spinning. Even though Griff had all of my attention, throughout the retelling of his afternoon I felt Phoenix's eyes boring into me from across the room. I didn't need to look to know he was staring at me. Likely to ascertain if I was going to blow a gasket.

I was nearing the redline when Griff's voice softened as he told me, "We saved 'em, Mom. They're here, in the barn. Wanna see 'em?"

No, I absolutely didn't want to see four beautiful animals that had been mistreated. Considering I bawled my eyes out at ASPCA commercials, especially the ones that had that Sarah McLachlan song playing, seeing abuse in real life would give me nightmares for a month.

"Sure, honey."

"Can we take my mom out?" Griff asked Chelsea.

"Of course."

"Can we show her Rebel, Gypsy, and Trigger, too?"

The sweetest pain I'd ever felt flowed over me. An ache that was really a longing at hearing the excitement in my son's voice—innocent and simple, just like the way he used to sound. A tone of voice I hadn't heard in so long I was afraid I'd never hear it again.

"I know," Sawyer put in. "Why don't we call in a pizza or something?"

"Sawyer..." Dylan muttered.

"What? I'm *starved*. I bet you're hungry, too, after all that hard work you did today."

"Baby," Dylan grunted. "You're killing me."

Unperturbed, Sawyer went on, "Chels, Shiloh, are y'all hungry?"

"Starved," Shiloh agreed.

"What do you like on your pizza, bud?" Phoenix asked.

Um.

What?

"Everything," my son answered.

And that was the truth. He liked everything, even anchovies and pineapple both separate and together along with whatever other combination of toppings.

"Babe?"

Again.

Um.

What?

My eyes darted around the room, and I found everyone staring at me expectantly.

"Cheese."

Phoenix's laugh rang out and I watched in fascination as he was transformed from a sexy brooding man to a sexy carefree man.

Had I ever heard him laugh?

No way. If I had I would've remembered, there was no chance I'd ever forget a sound so amazing.

When his laughter died down, he asked, "Seriously?"

"Why is that funny?"

"How is it possible your kid will eat anything on a pizza and you only like cheese?"

That was a question for the ages. Conor hated pizza with a passion. I'd eat it though it wasn't a favorite, but Griff loved it and would eat it every night if I'd allow it.

"No clue," I told him.

"I'm adventurous," Griff piped up. "Though jalapeño, pepperoni, fresh tomatoes, and garlic is my favorite."

Who was this kid and what had he done with my child?

"That sounds like something only a teenager can eat." Matt chuckled. "Go on out. I'll order and meet you in the barn."

Three men reached for their wallets, but none of them were successful.

"My house, my treat." Matt waved them off.

"Matt—"

"You bought dinner last time we were out," Matt interrupted Phoenix.

"Please don't pull the macho, alpha, swing your—"

"Sunny," Phoenix snapped and jerked his head in Griff's direction.

Shiloh gave her brother a dirty look before she turned to me.

"Do you have any brothers?"

"No."

"Lucky you. They're annoying," she huffed. "As I was saying, please don't pull the macho, alpha, swing your *money* around. You know Matt's never gonna let guests pay for dinner. And I am actually hungry. I missed my lunch because of a call-out and missed my midday snack. I'm getting hangry so I'd appreciate it if we could skip the arguing about who's paying, thank Matt for his generosity, and let him order dinner."

"For the record, we're not guests," Dylan put in. "We're intruders."

See? Confused.

My son and I were standing in a stranger's house. My boy was sounding and behaving like his old self. I'd gone from mildly annoyed that Phoenix had taken Griff with him to rescue horses without my knowledge to listening to my son tell a beautiful story. Meaning the anger slipped away but concern had crept in.

Now we were apparently staying for dinner.

I wanted to decline.

But I couldn't bear to break whatever spell Griff was under. I'd stay in that house forever if it meant I had my sweet, loving son back.

"Come on, we'll go out through the back," Chelsea began but stopped when she looked down at my feet. "What size shoes do you wear?"

Her question was so bizarre it took me a second to answer.

"Ten and a half."

"Damn, I'm a seven. You can slip on a pair of Matt's muck boots. They'll be big, but it'll be better than ruining those heels. And double damn because those are hot, and I'd love to borrow them. Not that I dress up much, I actually only own one pair of heels, but I'd totally break my neck to wear those."

The speed at which she rushed out that information was impressive. But that wasn't what struck me, neither was her calling my heels sexy and I had to admit they totally were. I rarely wore them because they killed my feet, but they did wonders for my ass. So, I made the concession once in a blue moon.

What hit me was her friendliness.

There was a time when I was outgoing and friendly, too. But that was before my ex-husband had been arrested. After his heinous crimes hit the news—clogging the airwaves and imploding my life—I had no choice but to become an introvert and keep to myself. Chicago was a large, bustling metropolis but it wasn't so big that after people saw my picture in connection to Conor, they didn't recognize me. And the people I'd worked with certainly knew who I was and what Conor had done and it didn't take them long to shun me.

Still, that didn't mean I wasn't friendly. I just was no longer outgoing and I'd gotten used to it. That was why I'd put off making friends after we moved.

Without waiting for me to respond—not that I had a response—Chelsea walked us through her beautiful home. I wanted to be nosy and look around, but I refrained mostly because I was freaked out at the situation as a whole but also because Griff was in front of me animatedly chatting with Shiloh.

I had never seen the third Kent brother, but if you'd put Echo, Phoenix, and Shiloh in a crowd and told some random person to pick the siblings out there was no doubt it could be done. Their resemblance to each other bordered on freakishly remarkable. Shiloh was as beautiful as her brother. The few times I'd seen Echo, he'd carried himself in a closed-off way which meant I wouldn't call him beautiful, but he was still totally hot.

"You're coming to lunch tomorrow, right, Wren?" Sawyer asked from behind me.

I briefly looked over my shoulder and asked, "I'm sorry, what?"

"Lunch tomorrow. Josie arranged it, right?" she clarified. "We were hoping we could meet with you today, but Josie got caught up with the contractors."

I had no idea who the "we" was in that explanation, nor did I understand why Josie hadn't mentioned that lunch tomorrow would include other people.

"Josie didn't mention…" I paused to find the right words to use that wouldn't make me sound rude. I was totally out of practice with this whole socialization stuff. I was like a recluse who still left the house to go to work and run errands but other than that I was a hermit.

"She didn't tell you that we'd all be there," Sawyer helpfully filled in though I now had more questions.

"Who all's going to lunch?"

"Quinn, Addy, Hadley, Lauren, me, Josie, and Chelsea."

What in the actual hell?

"Uh," I mumbled. "What?"

Sawyer sounded like she was struggling not to laugh. She was making these strange gurgling noises which made me wonder if maybe she needed the Heimlich maneuver or mouth-to-mouth resuscitation.

"I understand now why Josie didn't tell you."

I bet she did. I totally would've bagged on lunch if I'd known I'd be facing down an hour with seven women I barely knew.

No way could I do that in a social setting.

Baby steps.

I had to have a few more lunches with Vanessa and maybe a couple with just Josie. Cut my teeth on the friendship thing before I went whole hog.

"I'm...um..."

Crap, what was I?

"Caught off-guard and overwhelmed?" Sawyer once again helpfully finished my thought.

We stepped into a huge sunroom. Chelsea broke off to the right and opened a closet. Shiloh, Griff, and Luke continued out the back door. Griff didn't break stride or conversation to look back and see if I was still following. That both thrilled me and made me sad. He'd stopped needing me in any real way years ago, and there were times I was happy he was coming into his own and becoming more and more independent.

Then there were times I missed the days when he wanted to hold my hand or he'd look to me for comfort.

"Here." Chelsea held out a pair of black boots. Both of my feet could have probably fit in one.

"I don't think I'll be able to walk in these," I told her.

"Just shuffle your feet," Phoenix suggested.

"I don't think that'll work."

"Want me to carry you?"

If I had to guess, my mouth gaped open. I wasn't a hundred percent sure because it also felt like I'd pinched my mouth together. All I knew was Phoenix found my expression funny. This was bad. Very, very bad. Amused Phoenix meant he smiled, and good Lawd, this new smile was a doozy. Lips twitching, mouth curving, corners of his eyes crinkling. If it wouldn't have made me look like a total crazy person, I would've pulled out my phone and snapped a picture.

"I see you don't like that idea," he *wrongly* surmised.

I loved the idea of Phoenix picking me up, throwing me over his shoulder, and carting me off...to a bedroom. Being five foot ten had its disadvantages. The first and most important being it was a pain in the ass to find jeans that fit me lengthwise that were also not saggy around the crotch. The second was, due to my height I had big feet, and finding cute strappy sandals was damn near impossible.

The third and maybe worst drawback was that since I was not small, no man had ever scooped me up and carried me anywhere. Being a lifelong romance reader, that was on my top ten list of hot-sex stuff to try.

Sadly, I had yet to fulfill *any* of my top ten hot sex stuff.

"Wren?"

Crap.

"I'll just shuffle my feet."

When I was done changing my shoes, we hustled out of the house and I went back to my conversation with Sawyer.

"So, I'm curious what's lunch about?"

"I'm afraid if I tell you, you won't come to lunch and Josie will be mad at me."

Damn.

It would be so easy to fib and tell Sawyer there was nothing she could say that would make me bag on lunch, but like always I couldn't get myself to lie.

We were almost to the barn when I finally found the

courage to admit, "It's not that I don't want to have lunch with all of you. I'm just...awkward. And when I'm with people I don't know I either get really quiet or super talkative, there's no in-between. I used to have a lot of friends, then my ex-husband got..." *Shit.* "Into trouble, and once everyone around town found out I kinda retreated so I wouldn't have to hear about it. Now, I'm used to being alone all the time, so I don't know how to..." I clamped my mouth closed when I realized what an ass I was making out of myself.

I felt a big, warm hand on my lower back, and some of my tension ebbed. Not enough for me to relax but enough to take my mind off what an idiot I'd been since all of my concentration was now on how good it felt when Phoenix touched me. And how I no longer wanted to know what it felt like to have him touch me in other places—I *needed* to know. It was beckoning on the verge of necessity.

"I don't think that's awkward; I think that's normal," Sawyer nicely massaged the truth. "Besides, lunch tomorrow will be great. You'll get a front-row seat to the madness."

"Madness?" I asked as I glanced around Chelsea's backyard.

Well, it wasn't a backyard exactly. It was more of a big open yard with a fenced-in area I assumed was for her horses. Beyond that stretched more open land. And in front of me was a huge red barn.

Being from the city, living in a wide-open space like this would be a dream. No neighbors in sight. No traffic noises. Nothing. Just peace and quiet.

"Yeah, total madness. See, Addy's pregnant but hiding it. The problem is she has horrible morning sickness. It's amusing to watch her come up with reasons to excuse herself and use the bathroom."

I assumed the Addy that Sawyer was talking about was Addy Durum, the woman who'd started the fitness classes at the Hope Center. However, the woman I'd met in passing didn't strike me as someone who would hide a pregnancy. Addy was sweet as she could be.

"Why is she hiding her pregnancy?"

"Because her sister Quinn has been trying to get pregnant for a long time, so she doesn't want to hurt her feelings since her other sister Hadley is pregnant with twins, though she looks like she's got ten in there."

Twins? Good God. I only had one and there were times when I'd thought I was going to fall asleep standing up. I couldn't imagine having two infants, two butts to change, two mouths to feed, and twice as much laundry. Everything times two. No way, no how, twins would kill me.

"Anyway," Sawyer continued. "I need help and Josie suggested we talk to you."

I didn't ask what Sawyer needed help with, not when I could barely breathe when my boy came into view. My hand slipped into the pocket of my trousers, I pulled out my phone, engaged the camera, and held it in front of me, then snapped pictures of Griff.

Griffin stood in front of a very skinny horse stroking the side of its face. The horse looked like it was in heaven. So did my son.

"Oh my God," I gasped when a second horse came into view.

Much like the first, it was way too thin. I could see every rib.

"We brought three back here," Phoenix told me softly.

"The fourth was taken to an emergency vet. She was too far gone for Chels to care for her here."

"Worse?"

"Yeah, baby, way worse. When we got her to the clinic the vet weighed her as part of her intake, and she was six hundred and eighty pounds. That's over three hundred pounds underweight."

"Who would..." The lump in my throat prevented me from finishing my asinine question.

I knew who would do such a thing—a soulless, depraved person.

"Mom, come here."

The closer I got the more my heart broke.

Chelsea was standing next to Griffin and I was grateful she was watching out for my son. He'd never been around large animals before and while the horse didn't look like he had the strength to do more than stand I didn't want Griff to accidentally spook him.

"This one is Dasher," he told me. "He's an American Quarter Horse gelding. That means he's been castrated. Oh and he's bay, that's his color."

Another stab to my heart.

Another glimpse of my son.

"He's beautiful," I noted.

"Chels said that she'll be able to get the weight back on him, but it'll take a while. If she gives him too much at once he'll get sick."

I glanced over at Chelsea who was beaming at my boy.

"And the one Luke and Shiloh are petting is Simon. He's also a Quarter Horse but he's grullo."

I glanced over at the mousy white horse and took in his beautiful black mane and the dark gray markings on his lower legs and felt the left side of my chest squeeze.

"We gave them baths when we got here. They were covered in mud and shi...poop," Griff corrected himself. "They need to be brushed but Chels doesn't want to tire them out any more than they are."

That was the second time Griff had called Chelsea Chels and I wondered if she was okay with that.

"Griff was a huge help today," Chelsea praised. "He even mucked out a stall for me and threw in new bedding for King."

"King's an Arabian. He's in quarantine away from the others because he had maggots in his wound."

My stomach roiled at the thought of maggots.

I was hoping Griff had misunderstood when I asked, "Maggots?"

"King was left wearing a rope halter," Chelsea started. "One of the knots rubbed a sore. Unfortunately, the wound was left untreated."

The information was delivered in an even tone but I didn't miss the spark of anger behind her hazel eyes.

"Chels cleaned and flushed it, got the maggots out, put some goop on it, and gave him a shot of antibiotics. But he has to stay in his stall for a week."

I looked across the aisle and saw only one stall door was closed. I shuffled across the way and poked my head over the door. Lying in the corner was a brown horse that looked like he was speckled with a darker brown. He barely picked up his head before he plopped it back down.

Overwhelming rage came over me. Rage and disgust pulsed through me until it leaked out of my eyes and rolled down my cheeks.

Maggots.

Fucking maggots.

Unable to look at the malnourished horse any longer I pinched my eyes closed.

"Hey," Phoenix whispered.

His arm slipped around my shoulder and he turned me until my face went into his neck and his other arm slid around. Then he hugged me.

I did not hug him back. Not because I didn't want to wrap my arms around Phoenix and burrow in, but because my arms were trapped under his and he was holding me so tightly I couldn't move.

I heard a commotion in the barn. I also heard Griff mumble something, then it went silent.

Silent except for my hitched breath as I tried to control my tears.

"How bad was it?" I asked.

"Bad," Phoenix answered.

"What happened to the owner?"

"He was arrested."

"Good."

There was a stretch of silence and just when I was ready to tell Phoenix I was okay he spoke.

"Listen, I need to explain about today."

Explain? I thought Griff had done a good job of telling me play-by-play details of his adventure to rescue the horses.

"Griff already—"

"There's more."

Oh, no.

"More horses?"

"No, more to tell you."

Phoenix loosened his arms. One hand slid down to my hip, and his fingertips curled in.

"When we got there, Milo, the man who owned the horses, was holding a shotgun to Chelsea's back."

Holy shit.

Thank God Chelsea was okay.

Griffin.

"He didn't see," Phoenix rushed on. "I told him to stay in the truck while I went into the barn to check on the situation. She was in there to get a mare, Dory. That brings me to the next part. Chelsea was technically there to steal Milo's horses. She knows Milo's daughter from her rodeo days and this woman called Chelsea to tell her that her dad had these horses and wasn't taking care of them. The daughter doesn't have a trailer and asked Chelsea to go over and get them. Obviously, she did that, but Milo didn't want Chelsea to take them. They were in a standoff when I got there. My brother, a friend of mine who's also a cop, Ethan, and I were in the barn dealing with Milo when my sister, Luke, and Dylan showed up. Shiloh and Luke went to my truck to check on Griff. He got out and started helping them load up the horses into Chelsea's trailer."

I was stuck on the part about Chelsea having a shotgun pointed at her. When I realized Phoenix was waiting for me to respond I gave him the only one I could think of.

"Good."

"Good?"

"Yeah, good. I'm glad Griff helped load up the horses from that monster's house."

"Wren, technically my sister, Luke, and Dylan were stealing—"

"They were *rescuing*," I corrected. "But if you wanna be technical and call it stealing—good. I'm glad my son helped steal these horses. Hell, I'm proud he stole them. I'm so beside myself with gladness I feel like I'm gonna burst with it."

Phoenix did a slow blink, and when his lids were back to fully open something was working behind his eyes. He was scanning my face, searching. When he found what he was looking for he gave me a small smile.

"He's a good kid, Wren. He worked hard today. But beyond that, he gave three broken animals kindness. Says a lot about him. He told you they were covered in filth, but he didn't tell you it was caked on so thick they needed to be washed three times. And Milo's place reeked. Not to mention the flies were horrible. He didn't complain, he didn't bitch about the smell, he just got to work giving these animals what they needed."

Pride swelled, making the tears well to the brim.

"Good," I whispered.

I couldn't pinpoint the moment it had happened. I only knew that at some point Phoenix had allowed himself to come out from behind his fortress walls.

Seeing him like that was a blessing and a curse. A wicked curse that was slowly crushing my heart. A beautiful blessing with barbs and thorns that would slice me to bits if I allowed myself to fall.

Phoenix's hand on my lower back slowly slid up my spine. His fingertips dug in and all the while his face was inching closer to mine. I held my breath as his lips came down on mine. Feather soft, a slow glide over mine, just a brush. A sweet graze. I leaned in, my lips parted, his tongue swept in, and Phoenix kissed me.

That was the moment everything changed.

Every*thing*.

From a kiss.

No, not *a* kiss, the best kiss of my life. He tasted of the stuff dreams were made of. He kissed like a man who knew what he wanted, how he wanted it, and how he was going to get it. I fully participated in every glide, stroke, and touch but I was not in control. Not of our kiss and not of my own hands as they roamed his back, exploring. My brain had turned off and my body turned on. No thoughts—just touch and taste and feel.

A beautiful kiss that should've never happened.

Reality crashed in as fast as it had vanished.

Phoenix pulled away and the moment our lips broke apart he angrily growled, "Fucking Christ."

My body locked up in preparation. I was out there past my walls, exposed; I needed to hurry and get back to safety. I needed to pull myself together and rebuild the wall before he told me kissing me was a mistake. With the taste of him still on my tongue, that blow would be too painful to bear. I needed my armor.

"Phoenix—"

"Jesus, Wren."

I blinked away some of the haze and chanced a look at Phoenix. As soon as my eyes met his I startled. But if I thought seeing his eyes blazing with desire was enough to make me jolt, his hand coming up to cup my jaw had me trembling. And when his thumb traced the line of my lips, my already wet panties flooded.

Oh. My. God.

Phoenix Kent could be gentle. He could be sweet. But when he kissed, he possessed.

"We shouldn't—" His thumb pressed against my lips preventing me from telling him what we both knew was the truth.

"Maybe not, but we did. And I can't say I regret it and I can't promise it won't happen again."

Phoenix's head dipped closer and right before his lips touched mine his thumb slid away.

I made no reply.

At that point, anything I said was going to either be a lie or prove me the idiot I was when I begged him to kiss me one more time.

"We better get you in the house," he said. "And I need to find Griff so we can help Chelsea get these horses situated."

"I can help."

"Baby, you can barely walk in those boots."

Crap, he was right. Matt's boots were so big that even shuffling was hard. I wondered what my son and Phoenix's sister would think if he carried me back into the house.

"C'mon." He grabbed my hand and pulled me toward the door. Five shuffles later he muttered, "This is ridiculous." He let go of my hand and moved around until he was in front of me. "Hop on."

Hop on?

"What?"

"Hop on."

"You can repeat yourself as many times as you like, Phoenix, but I have no idea what you're talking about."

"Hop on my back. I'll give you a piggyback. Or I can carry you, your choice. But, baby, it took you a year to get out here and I don't want it to take another getting back."

"It didn't take—"

"Hop on."

Welp, it looked like I was getting a piggyback ride.

"Fine. But if you pull a muscle and are laid up in bed for a month don't blame me."

"If I'm laid up in bed for a month, I wouldn't blame you but I sure as fuck would require around-the-clock care." I was still trying to work out what he meant when he continued, "And that care would necessitate you finding someone to look after your boy."

Did he mean I'd be in his bed with him?

"Unfortunately, I don't have the letters M. D. after my name, so I don't think I'd be much help."

"Baby, I got a really great fuckin' kiss that tells me otherwise."

Phoenix thought I was a great kisser?

Lawd.

Flying high off the knowledge Phoenix liked the way I kissed, I hopped on his back. His arms hooked under my thighs, mine went around his neck, and I held on the best I could without choking him.

"Christ."

"Am I too heavy?"

"No."

"Then why'd you say 'Christ'?"

"Got your legs wrapped around my waist. Not the way I envisioned but goddamn I knew they'd feel good."

If he didn't stop with the sexy talk there'd be a wet spot on the back of his t-shirt.

"And just so we're clear, I've spent a lot of time thinking about your long-ass legs wrapped around me."

Yep, there was going to be a wet spot.

"You need to stop talking."

"I will as soon as you tell me you don't regret kissin' me."

"That defeats the purpose of you not talking."

"How's that?"

Lie, Wren, just lie. For once just open your mouth and tell a big, huge whopper and protect yourself.

"Because telling you that would mean I'd be thinking about our kiss, which would make me think about you liking how I kiss, which would lead to me thinking I like the way you kiss, which would make me think about how I didn't want you to stop kissing me, which would make me think you in bed with a pulled muscle and how I really wanna play doctor-patient with you and see if that old saying about kissing injuries really makes them real better, and thinking about all of that is not helping the throbbing between my legs. Neither is my crotch pressed on your back while you're walking and rubbing..."

Holy fuck.

I dropped my forehead to his shoulder and prayed for a quick and painless death.

"Go on, finish," he prompted.

I shook my head and stayed silent.

"What's rubbing, Wren?"

I shook my head again and pinched my lips.

Phoenix continued walking and my very sensitive center continued to rub against his back just enough to get me more excited but not enough to tip me over the edge.

Thankfully, the back porch was only steps away and my ride was almost over.

"For the record, I'm on board. Any time you wanna play doctor-patient I'm game to kiss you all over and you can tell me when I'm done if anything still hurts."

Something was hurting right then.

"I wanted to be the doctor," I blurted out.

"Baby, you can be anything you wanna be as long as when you're done I get those legs wrapped around me."

My legs that were currently wrapped around him convulsed and I was beginning to wonder if after years of no sex—and before that a shitty sex life—I suddenly had the ability to spontaneously climax.

"I see you like that idea."

I said nothing.

9

Without opening my eyes, I reached for my ringing phone on my nightstand, and without bothering to look at the caller ID, I answered.

"Yeah?" I muttered.

"Call-out."

Jesus.

"Fucking hell. What time is it?"

"A little after three," my teammate Dalton informed me, sounding just as unhappy as I felt.

"Text me the meet-up."

I was rolling out of bed when Dalton gave me more information.

"SWAT team's in play."

Jesus fuck me. A call-out in the middle of the night was never good, not that it was ever a good time when my unit got called out, but really bad shit always happened just before sunrise. Add in a SWAT team and shit had gone sideways.

"Shiloh?" I asked.

"Sorry, brother," Dalton mumbled.

Fuck.

This wasn't the first call-out I'd been on where my baby sister would be in attendance with her team, and I knew it wouldn't be the last. But every time I rolled up to a staging area and saw her kitted out my gut knotted. It was a double-edged sword—she was excellent at her job and along with my brothers, there was no one I'd rather have at my back than her. The issue was it was *her* team that went in first. If Shiloh's SWAT team was called in, she cleared my way.

"See you there," I grumbled and disconnected.

I was pulling on a clean pair of cargos when Dalton's text came through. Five minutes later I was in my truck driving to a Dollar General across town wondering how Griff was. He had yet to turn back into a teenage punk. Through dinner, he chatted animatedly while Wren watched him, with the saddest fucking look on her face I'd ever seen. She was smiling but there was an underlying sorrow I couldn't miss. A longing that awoke something deep inside of me—a recklessness that I was afraid would end in disaster, but that I could no longer ignore. Desperation to shield her and Griffin from further pain.

Then there was that kiss, the one that never should've happened, but now that it had there was no going back. The damage was done. I'd taken a bite out of the proverbial apple, tasted how fucking sweet it was, and now I was hooked. So sitting through dinner with her next to me—Griff directly across from Wren, and my friends filling in the rest of the chairs—had been torture.

And not because of the kiss. Not because she'd all but admitted she was getting off on me giving her a ride on my back. Not because those long, sexy legs of hers had been wrapped around me. Not because my dick had still been semi-hard at the thought of her playing doctor. Nope, all of that had contributed to my painful evening, but it was the way her leg had rested against mine throughout the meal. We'd had to scoot close to make room for everyone, but Wren purposefully made sure we were touching. Not only that but twice she'd adjusted her napkin on her lap and allowed her hand to brush over my thigh.

When dinner was over, she quickly said her goodbyes and rushed out the door with Griff. And last night when I called to check on her and make sure Griff was okay, she'd studiously avoided veering off the subject.

After we ended the call, I laid in bed with a stiff cock, but unlike all the other nights in the last month, I refrained from stroking off to one of many Wren fantasies. Part of the reason was I now knew my imagination paled in comparison. The other reason was one day soon I'd have the real thing.

The DG came into view along with an armored vehicle and plenty of marked and unmarked police cars. I pulled into the lot and found a spot and as soon as I got out of my truck, I did what I always did when I knew my sister's team was in play and I scanned the area. I found her across the lot standing with two of her teammates, Gordy and Valentine. Seeing them standing close did nothing to loosen my clenched jaw. Both men were exceptional at their jobs, both would lay down their lives for their team, and both respected and cared about my baby sister. But neither was bulletproof as Valentine found out when he took two bullets, one to the neck and one to the gut. That was the night my terror had grown exponentially. That was the night I was reminded that I wouldn't survive the loss of my sister. I'd made it through our mom leaving, our dad being locked up, and if something happened to Echo or River I'd be utterly wrecked. But if something happened to our Sunny, my brothers and I wouldn't recover. Echo was the glue that had held our family together, but Shiloh was the bond.

"Damn, brother," Dalton drawled. "You still look half asleep."

I glanced over at my friend and scowled. "And you look like you haven't gone to bed yet."

"Was just getting home when I got the call."

I didn't bother asking where he'd been. Dalton was a confirmed bachelor after a failed marriage to his high school sweetheart.

"Good night?" I asked and opened my back door to grab my gear and stalked to my tailgate.

"*Very* good night."

"Great, then you can take one for the team and run point tonight since you're so chipper."

All humor fled as he stepped closer.

"Talked to Cap." He jerked his head to the side and my eyes drifted in that direction. "We're here because word is, there's a large cache of weapons belonging to Jimmy Lonesome in the warehouse SWAT's gonna hit."

Suddenly I was wide awake. Jimmy Lonesome hit Georgia a few years back and made quick work of setting up shop in Hollow Point. He ran guns up and down the Eastern Seaboard. Recently he'd branched out and was trying to take over territory in Atlanta. Lonesome had to be taken down before Atlanta became a war zone.

"Who talked?" I asked.

"Low-level crew member but Cap says he thinks the guy's credible. When the detectives were interviewing him he gave up three guys, and when uniforms went to pick them up they were exactly where this guy said they'd be, and they had weapons and currency on them. SWAT's here to serve a warrant. V.P. of some motorcycle club outta Florida is up here making a deal. Our guy says that deal's going down tonight. If a deal's struck the crates of guns leave tomorrow."

My insides seized.

Not only were we dealing with the Lonesome Crew, but an MC was in play.

"How many club guys came up with their Veep?"

"Ten."

Jesus.

"Let me guess, they're all inside the warehouse."

Dalton nonchalantly shrugged.

He wasn't being a prick; it was what it was. This was our job and any other night, when my sister wasn't strapped preparing to kick in a door, I would've felt the same as Dalton.

Speaking of...

"Am I interrupting?" Shiloh asked.

I wondered how pissed she'd be at me if I cuffed her to the steering wheel of my truck.

I didn't need to wonder; there wasn't a word strong enough to measure that level of pisstivity.

"Nope," I replied. "Dalton was giving me a brief."

"Did he tell you Ocala changed up entry?"

Ocala was Shiloh's lieutenant. She worked out of the six-ten and Dalton and I worked out of the six-twenty-eight. Echo worked out of a different station as well. And before River moved to Idaho he worked a city over.

"Haven't gotten that far," I told her as I unzipped my bag and pulled out my vest.

"When Ocala was briefed and found out Lonesome's crew was hosting a party he called in Bravo."

"Hosting a party," Dalton muttered with a smile.

Shiloh grinned back, lifted her hands to her vest, and tucked her fingers under the Kevlar at the neck.

I tugged the Velcro strap and fastened it around my waist. As soon as I did, a memory came flashing back. Wren in her office eye-fucking the hell out of me. At the time I'd paid no mind to it, it was something that happened a lot. I knew I wasn't ugly and that wasn't me being a dick, it was just plain truth, but when I was in uniform women stared openly. I had never used my uniform to get laid. I knew guys who solely fucked badge bunnies. Dalton was not one of those men. Neither was I. Easy women did nothing for me. But, I'd have no problem wearing my uniform to Wren's house and changing up doctor/patient to warden/inmate.

"Um...brother...you listenin' to me?" My sister's voice pulled me out of my dirty fantasy.

Wren wearing my cuffs, bent over her bed, begging me to...

"Phoenix," Shiloh snapped.

"What?"

I cut my eyes to Dalton's stupid ass as he busted out laughing.

"Just announce to the world we're staging to knock in some doors," I sniped.

"We are ten miles away," he correctly noted. "And I don't know what you were thinking about but you're either plotting murder or that's your sex face. The first I'll take your back on, the second I'll take your back and tell you to get a new look. That one is scary as fuck and won't get you—"

"Please stop." Shiloh accompanied her demand with a gagging sound. "I like to think of my brother as a virgin."

"Yeah, and I bet he likes to think of you as one as well. Though you live with your man so—"

"Do not finish that," I growled.

"Damn, you two are easy to rile up."

"I'm gonna let you finish gearing up," Dalton started. "Meet up with you when you're done."

I gave Dalton a chin lift and went back to securing my kit.

"Be safe, Sunny."

"Always. You, too, Dalton."

Shiloh waited a beat before she announced, "I like her."

I stopped rummaging through my bag and slid my eyes to my sister.

"Who?"

"Wren."

"Sunny—"

"I really like her. So does Luke. And I'm already half in love with that boy. He..." she trailed off then began again in a whisper, "Reminds me of us. He's got a little bit of us inside of him."

I sucked in a breath just as the fire lit in my chest.

"This isn't the time to talk about this, but I wanted you to know. We like her and I talked to Echo. He knew about her, which wasn't surprising since both of you assholes like me to be the last to know anything. Which means when the time comes and I'm ready to give you nieces and nephews I'm gonna find out the sex of the baby and not tell either of you."

I was looking forward to the day my sister turned into the Virgin Mary and was impregnated by immaculate conception.

"Anyway, I was gonna put her through the paces like you did with Luke, but after you guys came out of the barn and she looked freaked out I figured you were doing a bang-up job of fucking things up with her and I didn't wanna make it worse. So I've decided I'm taking her back. Last thing I'm gonna say is don't fuck this up, Phoenix."

"Sunny—"

"Nope. Rule one, no arguing before door kicking."

Goddamn sneaky brat.

The Kent siblings had one hard and fast rule—no harsh words before work.

"Before you go back to your team, you know I love you, right?"

Shiloh's face gentled when she returned, "Down to my soul, big brother."

"Good. Now go to work and let me finish."

She didn't move and something crossed over her features that made me brace.

And thank fuck I did.

Shiloh reached out and grabbed my forearm, pulled my hand out of my bag, and used her finger to trace the letters of her name tatted there.

"You know what I want most in life?"

I wasn't sure I liked where this was going.

"What?"

"For my name to be covered with the woman's who loves you almost as much as I do."

She dropped my arm and gave me a smile.

"Kick ass tonight, big brother."

I had to swallow the lump in my throat before I could speak.

"Be smart."

"Always am."

With that, she walked off.

I glanced down at my tattoo and wondered what Wren's name would look like scrolled under my sister's. That was never going to happen; my sister would forever have my forearm.

No, Wren's name would be inked over my heart with Griff's just below it.

∽

"How can you possibly be hungry?" I grumbled and followed Dalton into the café.

"I haven't eaten since dinner last night, that's how."

Neither had I but I was officially a walking zombie. By the time we hit the warehouse it had been nearing five in the morning. It had taken thirty minutes to secure the targets, then another six hours of load out and paperwork. I didn't want food; I wanted my bed.

I heard my name called but in my groggy state, my brain wasn't firing on all cylinders.

"Hey, Phoenix." The voice registered and I glanced to the side to find Addy staring at me. "You okay?"

"Yeah, just coming off a call-out."

Addy was good friends with my sister and her cousin was a cop, so she was well acquainted with the ins and outs of police work. So when she did a full body scan I knew it was nothing more than a welfare check, not to mention she was very happily married and as previously noted knocked up.

When she was done with her perusal her eyes moved to Dalton.

"Sorry, I'm half asleep. Addy, this is my partner, Dalton," I introduced, then decided to clearly define boundaries and tacked on, "Dalton, this is Addy, my friend Trey's *wife*."

I heard Dalton chuckle, taking no offense to my clarification.

Dalton liked to get laid, and he liked it on the regular, but he did not ever cross that line, not ever. He didn't even skirt it with flirting.

"Nice to meet you, Addy."

"You, too, Dalton."

"Everything go okay?"

"Bad guys left in cuffs, good guys all went home, and the only blood shed was from those who deserved it."

"Excellent." She paused for a moment then started. "We're having lunch with Wren."

I had to be dog-ass tired to forget Wren was meeting with Josie and the other women. Last night, Sawyer never said why they were all having lunch, just that she needed Wren's help. I'd meant to call Wren this morning to reassure her that Addy, Hadley, Quinn, and Lauren were all good women and she had nothing to be worried about. But obviously, I hadn't done that.

I glanced around the crowded café and in the far corner spotted the group of women. Wren's eyes came up and collided with mine. There was no other word for it, the collision was immediate. It was physical—I *felt* her gaze. And if the way her shoulders jerked was any indication, she felt me, too.

"Who's Wren?" Dalton asked.

"A friend."

"What kind of friend?"

Possessiveness reared its ugly head.

"The kind that's off limits."

"Right." He chuckled. "Are we going to go over and say hello?"

"No, you're gonna go order your food and I'm going to go over and say hello."

Addy's eyes were ping-ponging between us.

"Sometimes it amazes me," she muttered.

"What does?"

"The way all you men behave the exact same way."

"What way?"

"Oh, you know, knuckle-dragging, over-protective, domineering, growly. I just have one question; what stage are we at?"

My sleep-deprived mind was not following.

"Stage?"

"Yeah, like are you two still circling each other? Have you admitted to yourself that you like her? Have you made your move or are you still in denial?"

"I have no idea what you're talking about."

"The denial stage always takes the longest," she mumbled.

Yeah, it was time to change the subject.

"Hey, how far along are you?"

Addy's eyes got comically round before they narrowed. "Don't start."

"How about I won't bring up you being pregnant and you drop whatever it is you're talking about?"

"Deal."

Thank fuck.

"By the way, congrats."

Addy's face lit and there she was—the sweet woman I'd come to know.

"Thanks."

"Anyone gonna let me in on what's going on?"

"It is too complicated to explain when I'm functioning at full capacity. Now, it would be impossible."

"Right."

"Go say hi to your woman, I'm ordering. Want anything?"

Yeah, Wren in my bed naked.

"No."

"Nice meeting you again."

"You, too."

Dalton wove through the bodies to get to the hostess stand and I followed Addy across the room. The closer I got to the table the wider Wren's eyes got and when I skirted the table to get to her side, my destination finally dawned on her.

"Hey, baby."

"Uh, hey, Phoenix."

I bent and kissed her temple, let my lips linger there, and whispered, "You look beautiful."

"You look exhausted, everything okay?"

"Long night."

Unable to stop myself I gave her another kiss before I straightened and addressed the table.

"Ladies."

As usual, it was Quinn who piped up first.

"Ladies? You come strolling over here like a man on a mission, beeline it to Wren, call her *baby*, kiss her—*twice*—and all you have to say is *ladies*?"

"Quinn," Lauren admonished.

"I'm with my sister on this," Hadley put in.

Of course she would be, she was the second in command of shit-talking Walker women. Even though they were all married off and no longer technically Walkers. Except Hadley; she was married but still a Walker. But that was a story for a different day and more complicated than why Addy wasn't celebrating her pregnancy with the people who loved her the most.

"My apologies."

"You're not sorry," Hadley grumbled. "I'm gonna need you to state your intention."

"I think his intentions are unholy." Sawyer leaned toward Hadley and whispered loudly.

"No shit. I know that look," Quinn rejoined.

Next up was Chelsea who was sporting a shit-eating grin that clearly communicated she knew my intentions and she'd seen firsthand at dinner that Wren was open to the idea of those being "unholy".

"So do I," Chelsea said.

"Me, too," Lauren added.

I glanced at Addy and found she was biting her lip, wanting to join in but not wanting me to spill her "secret".

"Where's Josie?"

"She already left. She had to get to the bank for a meeting," Sawyer explained.

That meant they'd been there awhile and were still sitting around chatting.

Good.

I was happy to see Wren socializing with the women.

I felt Wren stiffen next to me and looked down. She was staring across the restaurant with a smile that screamed secretive.

"Who are you looking at?" I asked with more force than was probably necessary.

Her gaze snapped back to mine, and she mumbled, "No one."

I glanced back across the room and saw Dalton waiting for me by the door with his eyes laser-focused on Wren.

What the fuck?

"Do you know my partner?"

Yeah, jealousy was a motherfucker, but I couldn't deny

the thought of my Wren having any sort of run-in with Dalton made my blood heat.

Women rarely turned him down.

"Your partner? Who's your partner?"

"Baby, you're looking right at him."

"Hot guy in the black tee is your partner?" she breathed.

Okay. Yeah. What in the actual fuck?

I felt my eyebrows hit my hairline when I asked, "Hot guy?"

"Oh my God. This is so awesome," she said and reached for her phone.

"Uh, Wren, you might wanna explain before Phoenix's head explodes," Chelsea helpfully suggested because yes, my fucking head was getting ready to detonate.

With her phone up and her fingers flying over the screen, she explained.

"I was having lunch with my friend Vanessa at this coffee place next to our office and she asked me if I believed in kismet. I thought that was a weird thing to ask until she explained that over the last few weeks, she'd run into the same guy five times."

When Wren's concentration on her phone became so focused she stopped speaking, I not-so-softly nudged her.

"And that has to do with Dalton, how?"

"Dalton, nice," she whispered and continued to type.

"Wren?" I growled.

"Jeez, big boy, keep your pants on. He's the hot guy, your partner Dalton. He was at the café when we were having lunch and she pointed him out."

"Just a thought, baby, but maybe you can stop calling him the hot guy," I suggested.

There was a round of laughter at the table, but I barely heard it when Wren finally looked up from her phone and narrowed those goddamned pretty eyes I couldn't get enough of on me and said, "Why? He's nowhere near as hot as you but he's still hot."

It took a moment for Wren to fully grasp what she'd blurted out but when she did her cheeks flamed red and her eyes widened.

"I mean—"

"Oh, no, Wren. No takebacks, baby. You said what you said."

Her phone chimed with an incoming text and I used that to excuse myself.

"I'VE BEEN UP since three. Gonna go home and catch a nap before I go pick up Griff."

"He can—"

"Baby, I promised him I'd pick him up and take him to Chelsea's and check on the horses and that's what I'm gonna do. I'll drop him off at home around six. But just to warn you, his homework won't be done."

Big blue eyes stared up at me.

Fuck, I really wished we didn't have an audience so I could give her a replay of the kiss we shared in the barn.

"Okay."

"See you later, baby."

When I didn't move, her head tilted to the side in a silent question.

I had nothing to say, and I had no idea why I wasn't leaving.

But I couldn't bring myself to move.

And the longer I stood there looking into her eyes, the more I swear I felt the needle of the tattoo gun piercing my flesh, permanently inking in the letters of her name.

Right over my heart.

She would be everything I needed.

And in return, I would be exactly who they needed.

"Sweetheart?"

"See you tonight, Wren."

"Tonight, Phoenix."

I was five steps away when I heard Quinn.

"I think you need to call out sick for the rest of the day because you have some explaining to do, sister."

That sounded like a stellar idea. But if Wren called out of work sick she would not be spending the day gabbing with the girls.

10

All eyes were on me.

I felt them. And the longer the women stared the more nervous I became.

"Is someone gonna say something?" I blurted.

"Um, we're waiting on you to say something," Quinn announced.

Damn, Phoenix!

Everything was going so well until he showed up. The women and I were chatting about my work, the work they did at Womens, Inc, about when the Hope Center would reopen. Phoenix had come up in conversation of course because we'd talked about Griffin and what he was doing after school now that he wasn't at the center. But that had been different. The conversation had revolved around Griff and Phoenix, not me and Phoenix. That didn't mean that Chelsea hadn't given me some side-eye glances, but she hadn't said anything. Not that there was much to tell, unless...

My gaze shot to Chelsea who was the only one not looking at me. Her eyes were firmly on the empty plate in front of her and her lips were pinched together like she was trying to physically hold back words.

Shit.

I opened my mouth but promptly closed it. I opened it again, but the lie still wouldn't break free.

Come on, Wren, lie.

You can do it.

Just say nothing's going on and everyone will move on, and we'd go back to talking about the grant proposal Sawyer needed help with.

"I can have something ready by next week," I said as nonchalantly as I could.

A very loud sputtering came from Chelsea.

"Does she honestly think that's gonna work?" Hadley asked the table.

"It seems like she does," Lauren put in.

"It's like she doesn't know us at all."

Well, I *didn't* know them.

"I saw Phoenix kiss her," Chelsea blabbed.

"Seriously?" Sawyer breathed. "I bet he's a good kisser. He looks like he'd be the kind of guy to just yank you to him and lay a hot and heavy smack-a-roo on you."

Did she just say, smack-a-roo?

"Oh, yeah, I can totally see that," Lauren agreed.

"I bet he gets that throaty growl mid-kiss," Hadley rejoined.

I was going to kill Phoenix.

And why had I agreed to this lunch in the first place? As soon as I'd found out lunch wasn't with Josie, it was with Josie and a gaggle of women, I should've backed out. But, no, I let my curiosity get the best of me and wanted to know what Sawyer needed help with.

Friending was too much. I needed to go back to having no friends. I needed to cut Vanessa out, too.

Vanessa, shit.

See, I totally sucked as a friend. I'd ghosted her in the middle of her excitedly texting me about her hot guy.

"Y'all are embarrassing her," Addy stepped in.

Thank God for sweet Addy.

"But this is Phoenix," Hadley defended.

"No, this is Wren and she's uncomfortable talking about this, so we need to back off before we scare her away completely."

Hadley turned to me and asked, "Are we scaring you off?"

That was a no-brainer.

"Kinda."

This time it was Sawyer who came to my rescue.

"I think Addy's right, we need to drop this. But before we do, I just want to tell you one thing." She paused and graciously waited for me to nod. "When we first started our program at the Hope Center, Josie gave us workups on all the kids to help us match the boys with the guys that were volunteering. Phoenix wasn't in the meeting when the guys were going through the files, but Echo was. He picked Griff for Phoenix. Actually, he demanded it. I don't know why I'm telling you that, except I thought maybe you'd like to know. I don't know Phoenix well, but I've watched them together and Phoenix cares deeply for Griff."

Sawyer had done more than watch my son and Phoenix interact, she'd been trapped in the locker room with them during the fire. She, too, had helped take care of my son. And since I didn't know what to make of Phoenix's brother demanding that Phoenix be the one to mentor Griff I latched onto something else.

"I know we've already talked about this, but it bears repeating. I appreciate what you did for Griffin."

"We were locked in that room together. We helped each other."

"You say that and I get it, but no offense—until you are a mother you can't fully comprehend what it means to me that you took care of my son and protected him. You didn't help him with his homework, Sawyer, you very literally saved my son's life. You, Josie, Phoenix, the firefighters. And in saving his life you saved mine. There's no repayment for that. I will forever be indebted to you."

Sawyer gave me a sad smile but nothing else, not that there was anything for her to say.

"Fine, I guess Phoenix's ultra-badass hotness is tabled until you come to learn that nothing is off-limits during lunch with the sisterhood." Quinn's gaze sliced to Addy before it came back to me. "But if by lunch three you're not giving us the juicy details torture might be employed."

Lunch three.

That was two more lunches.

Maybe I could do that.

I glanced down at my ringing phone. Vanessa, another reminder of a blossoming friendship. I declined the call, shot off a quick text that I'd talk to her when I got back to the office, and faced the group of women who had shown me nothing but acceptance and kindness.

"Here's the deal, I'm half in love with Phoenix. I have been for a while. I mean to say, I started falling in love with him before the fire. Maybe it was just the idea of him. But the more I watched him with Griff, the faster I started to fall. Then I chickened out and avoided him. He didn't like that. Now he's back and yes, yesterday he kissed me in Chelsea's barn. But maybe it wasn't the kind of kiss I needed it to be.

Maybe he just kissed me because he'd had an emotional day. I don't know, I'm trying to work that out. But I need to take this slow. As you are all aware my ex-husband isn't a good man. However, before he went to prison, he wasn't a good father. He constantly bailed on Griff. He never kept his promises. He lied all of the time. So I need to be sure Phoenix is who I think he is."

"What kind of kiss do you need it to be?" Addy asked softly.

"The forever kind. The kind of kiss that changed the very foundation of his life. The last first kiss. I need that kiss to mean to him what it meant to me and until I know that for sure I have to keep my heart safe."

"It was a forever kiss," Sawyer told me.

"You don't—"

"Trust me, Wren. Phoenix never, ever would've kissed you knowing what's at stake if that kiss didn't mean forever."

I wanted to believe that with every fiber of my being but still, I wasn't sure.

"What's at stake?"

"You. Griff. Everything," she returned.

Everything?

"Lunch one is in the books," Quinn announced. "We have to get back to work and so do you. But you'll think about helping with those grant proposals."

Work.

Yes, I could talk work all day.

"I'll have the first draft done by next week."

"That fast?" Sawyer inquired.

"Girl, I write grants for a living. I can do three a day if I have to."

"Wow. I've been working on the first paragraph for the last week. Josie was right, we should've called you a month ago. She said you were good, and you helped her secure a grant for the Hope Center, but she didn't say you were a freaking rockstar."

That felt great knowing that Josie had nice things to say about me.

Lunch wrapped up in a whirl of see-you-laters and *hugs*. At first, this made me a little uncomfortable but by the time I made it to Addy and she gave me a tight squeeze while murmuring, "I got your back. Take all the time you need," I gave the last two hugs far less stiffly.

I figured that sweet Addy could be a pit bull if needed.

I started toward the parking lot when Chelsea fell into step next to me.

"I'm parked on this side, too," she told me. "Griff was a... what the hell?"

Chelsea's abrupt change had made my steps falter and my eyes shot to her.

"What?"

"What the actual hell?" she hissed.

I didn't know what the actual hell. I didn't know anything and when I looked around the parking lot, I still didn't understand what the problem was. A woman was walking across the tarmac holding a toddler's hand and an old man was walking in our direction.

"You have twenty-four hours to return—" the old man started but Chelsea shouted over his demand.

"You should still be in jail!"

"I want my—"

"Fuck you," she spat.

Holy crap, Chelsea looked like she was going to fight the old man.

"Fuck you, *fuck you*, and fuck you some more. One more day with you and she would've been dead. Is that what you wanted? One more day, asshole. And the others weren't far behind her, so I don't care what you want but you're taking them back over my dead body!"

Oh my God, Chelsea was talking about the horse.

This was him. This was the monster who had neglected his horses.

Suddenly I hoped Chelsea kicked his ass. Hell, I wanted to help her kick his ass.

"Yeah, girl, that's the plan."

The man's threat sent a chill up my spine until I was frozen solid.

"Whatever, Milo. Those beauties are mine now and I got the paperwork from animal control that says so. Next time I see you it'll be in a courtroom."

Chelsea grabbed my arm and yanked.

She stopped by a pickup truck and let go.

"God," she exhaled. "I can't believe they let him out so soon. The vet said that was the worst case of neglect she'd ever seen and now he's just out. Can you believe that shit?"

No, I couldn't but I didn't know how the court system worked and I wasn't going to suggest to Chelsea that he'd made bail.

"He threatened you," I reminded her.

"That wasn't a threat," she denied. "That was an old man pissed off his horses were taken. He's an asshole and now everyone will know what he's done."

"Chelsea—"

"What's he gonna do? He's too old to fight me. Legally I'm in the right. There's nothing he can do to get his horses back. They're mine."

She was correct, he was too old to physically harm her. As noted, she could very easily kick his ass if he so much as lifted a hand to touch her.

"But Phoenix told me he had you at gun point," I reminded her.

"He did," she nonchalantly agreed like it was no big deal she'd had a gun pointed at her. "But he didn't shoot me. He didn't even discharge it to scare me. It was all for show. I've known his daughter for a long time. I know Milo; he's a grumpy, mean, son-of-a-bitch but he wouldn't shoot anyone."

Yeah, I thought that about my ex-husband, too, until he killed a man.

"But, I'll still tell Matt what Milo said," she gave in.

That made me feel a thousand times better. Matt didn't strike me as a man who would let a threat slide.

"Any word from the vet on how Dory's doing?"

Chelsea's expression softened and sadness crept into her eyes.

"Not well. They're doing everything they can for her."

Damn.

"I'm sorry," I muttered my understatement.

"So am I. Back to what I was saying, Griff was a big help yesterday and I know I told you at dinner last night, but he's welcome anytime. I could use the help and it's my experience that animals have a way of mending the soul. At least for me they always have."

I wanted to ask why she needed her soul mended but I refrained.

"Thanks, he'd love that."

"Right, I have to get back to the bar but it was great having lunch with you. And please don't let us scare you off. We're loud and crazy and a little nosy but we mean well. I guess what I'm trying to say is you be you and let us in at your pace. Quinn will likely push but she'll do it because she cares. And that's the thing about all of them, they love hard. You can't find a better group of women."

And Chelsea, she loved hard, too. Not just with her human friends—the care she'd shown those horses told me everything I needed to know about her.

Plus, I had a feeling she was right, there would be no better group of friends. That was, if Vanessa was added into the mix.

I'd get the lay of the land, then I'd invite Vanessa to lunch with us.

"We'll set up another lunch soon."

"Perfect!" Chelsea beamed.

Yeah, perfect.

I could totally do this friendship thing.

11

"Don't tell my mom I said this, but I think she has a hoarding issue," Griff muttered as he pulled down a box. "You should've seen all the crap she got rid of before we left Chicago. And yet we still have all of this."

Griff swept his arm wide indicating the boxes scattered around the garage floor.

He'd barely taken a breath before he went on, "She's got like every drawing I've ever drawn and every report card. It's crazy! Why does she save all this? She even had some noodle necklace I made her from kindergarten."

One could say that over the last week Griff had become talkative to the point where he rambled like his mother. I couldn't say I disliked hearing the kid tell me about his day, however, he left no room for comment.

He rolled up to his toes and reached for the last box on the top shelf with his fingertips.

"Let me get that one."

"I got it."

Before I could step around the stack of boxes in front of

me Griff jumped to knock the box off the shelf and stretched his arms as high as he could, but it wasn't enough to save the box from falling onto the concrete and spilling open.

Wren wasn't a fan of tape. Instead, she'd folded the flaps of the boxes into themselves, not the best way to store valuables in a garage if you didn't want bugs and mice to get into them.

"What the hell?" Griffin spat.

I looked down at the contents of the box and froze.

"What the fuck?" Griff yelled as he used the tip of his shoe to push around the photographs.

"Griff—"

He knelt down, went to his knees, scooped up a handful, and shouted, "Why the fuck does she have these?"

"Griffin! Stop!"

The kid didn't stop. He crumpled the photographs and threw them to the side.

"Why?" He was leaning forward sliding the pictures on the concrete.

Griffin and Conor.

Griff as a baby, as a little kid. In some of them, Griff looked a few years younger than he did now. Lots of fucking pictures of him and his dad. In some Griff had on a basketball uniform, a few were at a beach, one at a fair or carnival.

Pictures.

Jesus fuck.

Sour hit my gut and memories flooded.

I blinked but couldn't stop my vision from hazing over. Wren's garage faded into my childhood living room, Griff's angry heavy breathing turned into my sobs, and pictures of Conor morphed into images of me and my mom.

So many damn pictures of me, Echo, River, and Shiloh. Some of them were family pictures with our parents. Some with just me and my dad, Shiloh and my mom, River and my dad. So many pictures. My father ripping them and throwing them around the room while Echo tried to rescue some of them from my father's wrath.

That was it, that was all we'd ever have of our mother and Lester was destroying them all.

That was it.

Just those pictures, those memories captured in a photograph.

I'd never wondered why our mother hadn't loved us. Shiloh did, she wondered. It had eaten at her well into adulthood. River was the logical one; he'd understood that our parents' dysfunction was not his. Echo was the caretaker, the giver, our savior. He didn't have time to struggle with his own emotions because he was too busy managing ours. I was the one who couldn't navigate my feelings for our father.

Echo had been right. I had a different father than they did. I had a man who showed me he loved me. Not all the time, not even often, but enough that I clung to it. Then he'd treat my brothers and sister like shit, and I'd feel guilty for loving him. The cycle never ended until he was carted off in cuffs. Then he'd discarded me in favor of fucking with Echo. He'd send us letters, get us upset, and Echo would haul ass to the prison and tell him to knock it off. That cycle continued as well.

Over and over, Echo protected us.

Why the fuck couldn't I stop loving Lester?

Fucking shit.

The man was the worst kind of man, yet I wanted the motherfucker to love me so badly I couldn't stop fucking hoping.

Jesus.

"I hate him!" Griffin's painful sob yanked me back into the present.

I reached down and hauled Griff to his feet. Without warning, he moved. The violence in which his body collided with mine was shocking, the strength of his arms wrapped around my waist more so. But it was the way he burrowed his face into my chest that caused the most pain.

"I hate him," he repeated.

I wrapped my arms around him and told him the truth. "Bud, you don't and that's okay."

"I fucking hate him."

Christ, how many times have I said that?

"Griff, you don't and that's okay."

His arms turned to steel bands when he asked, "Why does she have those?"

I'd once asked my brother that same question when I found the box of pictures he'd saved from my father's tantrum.

"One day you'll want those memories, Griff."

"I don't want to remember anything about him."

I closed my eyes, rested my chin on the side of his head, and gave it to him straight.

"I've spent more years than you've been alive denying that I love my dad. I've forced myself to forget all the good memories. I've worked hard to push any love I have for him away because how can I love a man who took a life? How can I love a criminal?"

Accusation dripped from Griff's tone when he asked, "How can you?"

Jesus fuck, my heart hurt. It felt like all the shattered pieces were being torn out of my chest and one by one they were piercing my skin.

"I don't, Griffin, but I love the man who taught me how to change a tire."

With my admission, all the oxygen left my lungs until I was forced to inhale. "I love the man who sat next to me and watched TV." Thank fuck Griff was holding on to me or I might've crumbled. "I love the man who taught me how to ride a bike. That's the man I love."

Griff shoved in closer, which was to say, he was plastered tightly against my chest. His arms were wrapped tightly around me and I knew he could feel me shaking.

"Never told anyone that," I whispered. "Never had the courage to admit it. I hate the cop killer but I love my dad and there will come a time, son, when you will have to be honest with yourself. Not for him, not for your mom, but for yourself. Hate eats at your insides, it rots away the good. And one day those pictures will mean something to you."

I could no longer feel my body trembling, Griffin's sob erupted, the convulsion so strong I rocked back on my feet and braced.

It was corny as fuck and I'd never admit this to my brother but, at that moment, holding on to Griffin, all I could think about was, what would Echo do? What would he say? How would the man who was my brother but really my dad lead this boy to healing?

Echo was the best man I knew, the person who gave me every tool I needed to become the man I was. But there was no denying I'd taken what I could from Lester—the smallest, sliver of the good he had in him—and kept it for my own.

"I don't want those pictures," he muttered through his tears.

"I get that, and right now we'll put them away and you

don't need to look at them. But trust me—one day, you'll want them."

"How do you know?"

I slowly let go of Griffin and he followed suit, letting his arms fall away. Once we were untangled I stepped back and pulled my wallet out of my back pocket and flipped it open.

It wasn't easy to get out, tucked behind all my cards. But it was there, where it had always been.

I unfolded the picture and handed it to Griff.

His gaze immediately dropped to the photograph and his eyes widened.

"Is that you in the middle?"

"Yep. Me, Echo, River, Shiloh, my mom and my dad."

With his head still bent, just his eyes came to mine and he whispered, "I'm not ready."

"You don't have to be."

"I'm glad my mom changed my last name."

Fuck, did I get that. There had been times when I'd wish like fuck Echo had changed our last name from Kent.

"Hear me, son, you can feel whatever you want to feel. And it's okay for those feelings to change. What's not okay is not giving yourself permission to feel them. I've had a long time to come to understand that I can both love and hate someone. You're fourteen. This is fresh, it's gonna take time, but don't destroy something you can't ever get back, yeah?"

"Yeah."

With a long exhale, I nodded.

"I'm gonna clean these up. Do me a favor and go make sure we didn't miss the timer on the oven."

"It would suck if the lasagna was burnt and we'd have to go out for tacos."

"Right, that'd totally suck."

Griff handed me back the picture but before he could leave, I stopped him.

"One thing. I get you're pissed. I understand that seeing what you saw made something inside you snap, but watch the f-bombs. You know your mom doesn't like you cussing."

"Yeah, okay."

"Good. Go check on dinner. Your mom's gonna be home soon."

The kid said nothing, but his smile said it all.

I waited for him to go into the house before I looked down at the picture.

A precious memory.

I couldn't say we were ever a happy family in the traditional sense, but there were moments like the one in my hand. Everyone smiling, even my dad.

And maybe, just fucking maybe, there was a little bit of love.

12

It was funny how sometimes change was immediate and sometimes it slowly shifted.

In the last week, I'd experienced both.

Phoenix had become a fixture in our lives. Out of the last eleven days, I'd seen him for nine of them, which meant Griff had spent a lot of time with him, too. The only two days he missed spending time with my son were one day when he had something going on at work, and last Sunday. I figured he missed last Sunday because he needed a day to himself without a teenage boy tagging along.

Phoenix being around nearly every day had an immediate impact on Griffin. I was still riding the high of having my good-natured, helpful son back. But as good as that felt the guilt was also immediate.

Phoenix made all the difference, and as much as I tried not to think about all the things I'd been failing to provide my child, it was hard not to dwell on my shortcomings. And that guilt had been eating away at me until I broke down and pulled out the letters that Conor had sent, the ones that Griff found and read.

As an aside, Griff had apologized for reading them and for snooping in my nightstand. Though when he told me, he said he'd been looking for an extra charging cable—I did indeed keep many of them in the table next to my bed. He wasn't exactly snooping as much as he'd invaded my privacy.

So with that conversation out of the way—which went a hell of a lot better than any of our discussions in the last year—I sat down on the edge of the bed and read all of the letters. That was all it had taken for my guilt to melt away.

It was not my fault Griff was left without a father. I didn't take Conor away from my son. Conor murdered a man. My actions didn't force us to move. My actions didn't harm my child. I was not a perfect parent but reading those letters reminded me I was a damn good mother. I loved my son and deep down I knew he understood how much. He knew how hard it was for me to leave my old job. How hard it was to pick up and move to another state. It was difficult for both of us.

There wasn't one word in any of those letters that was worth a damn. There was no apology to our son. There was no accountability. Every word was total bullshit.

I should've read them as they were delivered. It would've saved me months of agonizing over my choices and all the things I was doing wrong.

I was not the fuck-up, Conor was.

I was not a failure, Conor was.

I was doing the best I could with the mess he'd left.

And one way or another my son and I would pull through. We'd get to the other side. We'd been happy once and we would find our way back there.

Fuck Conor.

"Ma?"

I smiled at the soapy bowl in my hand.

Not Mom—Ma. What he used to call me before we moved to Georgia.

"Yeah?"

"Is it cool if I go to the movies with Pierce and Austin?"

Oh, yeah, we were gonna be fine. Better than fine, we were getting back to great.

"Phoenix is coming over for dinner," I reminded him.

"I thought that was tomorrow after we fixed the back gate."

"Nope. That's today."

I waited for an argument that never came.

"If we see a late movie, is that cool with you?"

That was it, he'd change his plans.

I thought about all the hours my son was putting in at Chelsea's helping take care of the horse they'd rescued. He came home from cleaning out stalls exhausted then sat down and did his homework. His teachers had all emailed me to tell me he was caught up on his work and his grades had improved. His room was clean by teenage-boy standards, he'd kept up with his laundry, and he did all of this without a fight. And to my great delight, he'd cleaned his mouth up at home. I was under no illusion he didn't curse around his friends, and I'd let a few minor cuss words slip here and there but "fuck" absolutely not. And since that blow-up with Bill, he hadn't dropped a single F-bomb.

With all of that in mind, I made a decision, one that meant I'd miss seeing Phoenix.

"No, don't change your plans. The gate can wait. Do you need a ride?"

"Really? Are you sure? I can do the gate and then go."

I leaned my stomach against the counter in an effort to balance myself.

I really hoped my Griff was back to stay.

"Yeah, honey, I'm sure. Go have fun with your friends."

"Okay. And Austin's mom can pick me up and Pierce's mom can get us from the movies and bring me home."

"Sounds good."

I rinsed out the bowl and was preparing to place it in the strainer when I felt Griff slide up next to me.

He dropped a kiss on my cheek and muttered, "Thanks, Ma."

I waited until he was out of the kitchen before I dropped my head and closed my eyes. I tried but failed to keep the tears at bay.

∽

I WAS CURLED up in the corner of my couch, my eyes riveted to the TV and the insanity that was playing out on the screen. I wasn't big on watching television but with Griff gone to the movies, I decided on a lazy day and started flipping through the channels. I stopped flipping when I saw Lisa Rinna on the screen. Then I had to check the guide because I was unclear why exactly I was watching. *The Real Housewives of Beverly Hills*. Of course, I'd heard of the show because hello everyone who didn't live under a rock had heard of it, but I'd never watched it. Now Lisa was yelling at Kathy Hilton—I had to pause the show and Google Kathy Hilton because I didn't know who she was. When I resumed the show, I found Paris and Nicky's momma had a mouth on her and she waved her hands a lot when she was angry. But Lisa was having none of it. This shit was better than a soap opera. It was crazy. I couldn't believe people actually behaved this way. And not just people but wealthy people who were supposed to exhibit some class. I was thinking about popping some popcorn and going back to episode one and binging the whole series—one of the great things about coming into an older show, you could watch the season in one go—when my front door opened.

I pulled my gaze from the TV thinking Griff was home. However, it was not my son walking in, it was Phoenix.

Now my eyes were riveted on him so hard that I couldn't find my voice.

I had texted him that Griff was going to the movies with some buds, and we needed to reschedule the back gate and dinner.

Now he was here. Not only that but he'd let himself into my house.

He was almost to the couch when I asked, "Didn't you get my text?"

It was a ridiculous question since I knew he did because he'd answered with, "okay."

"Yep."

He didn't stop advancing so I felt it prudent to ascertain exactly what was going on.

"Then you know Griff's not here."

"Yep."

His big body stopped beside the couch, effectively blocking my view of the Lisa-slash-Kathy feud. I leaned my head back on the cushion and tipped my eyes way up but I didn't get a chance to do more than that before the blanket I was curled up in was torn off and tossed aside.

"Phoenix—"

"Baby, what the fuck are you wearing?"

Oh, no.

Ohmygod.

No.

I closed my eyes and pretended Phoenix was not

standing next to my couch while I was in my rattiest, most comfortable pair of sweats complete with bleach stains down the legs. And if that wasn't bad enough, I was wearing an extra-large Ren and Stimpy t-shirt I'd had for at least two decades, maybe three. The length of time I'd owned the tee was irrelevant, the mere fact it had cartoon characters on it plus it had been washed so many times it was not only thin but had holes in it meant it should've been thrown away a long time ago. But it was super soft and extra big which made it extra comfy so I'd kept it.

Now I wish I could rewind time, pass right on by Hot Topic, and never purchase the stupid shirt.

"You're not supposed to be here," I reminded him with my eyes screwed shut.

"Baby, is that a fuckin'... I don't know what those creatures are supposed to be. Are they bumping asses?"

Yes, yes, they were. Ren and Stimpy were bumping butts and if the shirt weren't bunched up he'd see that above them it said *Happy Happy Joy Joy*.

My life was now complete.

I could die now and know what true, honest-to-God mortification felt like.

"I don't wanna talk about my shirt."

"I feel the need to steal that when you're not lookin' and put it out of its misery."

There would be no need. As soon as he left, I was taking it off and throwing it in the trash.

"Why are you here?"

"Griff's not here."

I knew that, which was why I was so confused.

However, I quickly became less confused when Phoenix continued, "Was at the gym working out. When I was done, I decided it was time for you to play doctor."

I forgot I was dying of embarrassment and my eyes shot open.

He was staring down at me, all vestiges of his shield gone. I'd seen traces of it here and there but for the most part, when Phoenix was with me and Griff, it was gone. He'd also started giving me hugs before he left and temple kisses. Lots of temple kisses. But there'd been nothing beyond that, not even mild flirtation. I figured that he realized what happened in the barn was a mistake and he was moving us along as friends. That was disappointing but safe. And with all the changes in my life, safe was good. Safe was safe and I thought it wise to keep what had happened a one-time thing.

Now he was here, and he wanted to play doctor?

My body screamed *yes!*

My brain whispered *caution*.

"Baby, I told you it was going to happen again."

He had. In the barn, he said he didn't regret kissing me and couldn't promise it wouldn't happen again. But it hadn't.

"You pulled back," I accused.

"Damn right, I did," he admitted. "There's only so much a man can take. And that night at dinner I found with you it doesn't take much before I'm at my limit. I'm trying to build something with Griff. I don't need him walking in on me with my tongue in your mouth or worse, my hand up your shirt. He's getting back on track, and I wouldn't do anything to derail that. So, I pulled back and kept my distance until I could get you to myself. Now Griff's at the movies and I get you to myself. We only got a few hours—which sucks we gotta rush this, but I'll make it up to you when he feels comfortable enough to stay with my brother or sister. Hell, he's almost there with Chelsea and Matt."

There was so much there my head was spinning with information overload.

"You're building something with Griff?"

I don't know why I asked that because I knew he was. But more importantly, Griff knew.

"Yeah, and after a rocky start, we're getting where we need to be. I'm getting time in with Griff. Now I need time with you."

"I'm confused."

"I can see that, but in about ten minutes when my mouth is between your legs you'll be less so."

"Phoenix, that's the part I'm confused about."

"No, Wren, you're not confused, you're scared. Same as me. We move this to where we both want and it goes bad, we got Griff caught up in this. But if we stay where we are right now there's no chance of things getting fucked between us."

Holy shit.

We got Griff caught up in this.

We.

Phoenix's concern was Griff.

Not even Griff's own father had ever shown that much concern for my son.

"Right. Exactly."

"So, we stay where we are keeping those walls up between us because we're too fuckin' scared to move forward in a way that's good for all of us. Been living that way my whole life and, baby, that's not protection, that's captivity. Never really thought about it until I met you and Griff. Never wondered why I was so fucking lonely living in my own little world, keeping everyone away, not trusting anyone but Echo, River, and Shiloh.

"Another reason I retreated and didn't push sooner—I needed to be sure I was ready to step out and start living.

Griff deserves a fuckuva lot more than a half-assed, broken man. Can't say that in two weeks I'm healed, but I can tell you I'm no longer hemorrhaging. I won't lie and say I'm all that fired up about telling you about my shitty childhood, but I will. I'll tell you whatever you need to give you peace of mind.

"Griff's asked questions. It's getting easier to talk to him about it, but it's still not a topic I want to discuss. Other than my fucked-up parents I got no other baggage. Since I've been an adult, I haven't done anything I'm truly ashamed of. I'm an open book."

I won't lie.

I believed that. Phoenix was honest.

So fucking lonely.

I hated that he was lonely.

I needed to be sure.

I'm no longer hemorrhaging.

I'm an open book.

I vowed right then never to ask him about his parents. If he wanted to talk, I'd listen. But I didn't need to know anything beyond what he'd told me.

"My father had a drinking problem," I blurted. "And a gambling problem. And a problem with having sex outside of his marriage. He's also a habitual liar. I never lie, not even a white lie. My mother is a bitch. She hated my father before she divorced him, and she hates him even more now. She never hid that and talked shit about him all the time to me. That's why even though I despise Conor I will never say anything bad about him. I know how that feels and it hurts. Even if I hate my dad, I didn't need to hear my mother talk shit about him. I hardly talk to them. And I don't allow them any contact with Griff. That's all about them."

I sucked in a breath and rushed to finish, wanting to get this over with so I never had to talk about this again.

"I met Conor when I was nineteen. I got pregnant and we got married. He said all the right things, did all the right things, and had all the right answers—but they were all lies. After we were married and Griffin was born, it was like he was a different person. He stopped pretending and when he wasn't faking at being nice he was a total dick. The only reason our marriage lasted as long as it did was because he was a workaholic. He cared more about money and getting ahead than he did about us. I would've admired his ambition and supported him working eighty hours a week if he hadn't come home smelling of perfume and booze. That was when I realized I'd married my father so I left him. Griffin was four. After that, he was a shit father who rarely saw Griff."

Next came the hardest part.

"Then he murdered a client. The guy wanted out of a contract, so Conor killed him. Not just killed him but thought it out, planned it, followed the man for weeks, followed his wife, totally premeditated. Well, he thought about how to kill the guy, but he didn't think about Griffin and how his life would change. Didn't think about the man's widow and kids or the rest of his family. Conor simply did what Conor does best and acted like a selfish asshole."

But I was wrong about it being the hardest part. The hardest part was admitting the truth about myself.

"I overthink and dwell on my choices because no one in my life ever paid attention to the significance of their actions. Not my parents and certainly not Conor. Everything has always been left up to me and I'm deathly afraid of making the wrong choice and harming my son."

When I was finished, Phoenix's expression hadn't changed. There was no judgment or disappointment.

"You done?"

I thought about his question and if there was anything else I needed to add. But that was it, that was my life in a nutshell. It needed no expansion. My parents were not good parents. They taught me all the wrong things and I thought that said it all. Conor was who he was, and I had nothing to add to that. I'd been divorced for ten years—no further processing required.

"Yes," I said.

"Good."

Then suddenly I was no longer curled into the corner of my couch. Phoenix had bent forward and plucked me right out. However, I wasn't on my feet. He was cradling me in his arms, stalking through my living room.

Cradling me.

Holy crap.

I didn't get a chance to fully appreciate the moment, with my heart pounding and my mind racing, the walk to my room was a blur.

Phoenix tipped his arms and let me down gently until I was on my feet next to my bed. His hand came up and went around the back of my neck, keeping me steady.

He leaned in close and in a fierce whisper he vowed, "I will never lie to you, Wren."

The fullness of his promise weighed heavy. My heart was no longer pounding. It slowed to a tired beat, a slow, calm thump. Yet that was impossible when it felt like it was going to explode out of my chest.

His hand slid up into my hair, he gently tugged, and asked, "You hear me?"

"Yes."

"No walls."

That scared me to death.

"No walls, Wren," he repeated. "Nothing between us. You're safe with me."

His deep scowl and harsh tone were a stark contradiction to the sweet promise.

"You're safe with me, too."

"I know."

He knew.

No hesitation.

"We're done talking," he announced.

And to make that official, his mouth came down on mine and his fist tightened in my hair. Unlike the first time he kissed me, Phoenix didn't coax his way in. He kissed me like a man named Phoenix Kent would. He took ownership of that kiss, in a way that left no room for doubt.

I'd never been kissed dizzy before. I'd been well on my way to dizzy in the barn, but he'd pulled back before I went mindless.

But not this time.

I was dizzy with his kiss, my desire so overwhelming I went wild. My hands clawed at his shirt, but I quickly gave up on that and went for the button of his jeans instead. I had them undone, getting close to the good stuff, when he grabbed my wrist and broke the kiss.

No!

"How attached are you to this shirt?"

My shirt?

"I'm not."

I was so fascinated by the change that came over him, the way his blue eyes deepened, the way they could be fiery and soft at the same time, I missed his hands coming up.

The sound of fabric tearing rent the air and my body jerked.

I lost his eyes when they dropped to my bare chest.

"Jesus."

From there everything went out of control.

My ratty-assed sweats and panties were around my ankles, his shirt was off and tossed aside, his jeans landed next to his shirt, and then I was flat on my back in my bed when he tugged my sweats free.

"Spread."

I spread.

He dropped to his knees next to my bed, grabbed my ankle, and tugged me to the edge.

I had yet to recover from the full-body quake he induced when he set my leg over his shoulder, turned his head, and kissed the inside of my thigh.

Phoenix's eyes tipped up to meet mine as his head dipped down, which meant he was watching me as he dragged his tongue all the way to my center.

Okay, that was hot.

So freaking hot, my hips bucked.

Phoenix rightly took that as encouragement.

He needed none after that.

With his mouth between my legs, his tongue working my clit, and his eyes glued to mine I had an out-of-body experience. Every inch of my skin was burning, my breasts ached, my pussy convulsed, and my lungs burned from panting. I was so close to tipping over into bliss my back arched, and my head hit the bed.

"Watch me."

His growled command vibrated against my clit.

It was too much.

I shook my head and fisted the comforter.

"Watch. Me. Wren."

I slowly lifted my head and watched.

Phoenix was not slow. He licked and sucked until my hips were off the bed and I was grinding myself against his mouth.

This time there was no stopping my orgasm. It bowled me over. It overtook all thought. Mindlessly my hands came off the bed, I reached for Phoenix's head, and gripping his hair I fucked his face. His grunts and growls cut through my delirium. I heard him but I was too far gone to comprehend anything beyond the pleasure rippling through me.

Phoenix arched back, pulled his head free, and got to his feet.

The sight of him cut through the haze and I greedily took him in. The first time I saw him without a shirt I didn't allow myself to stare. I'd blocked the image from my memory the best I could. This time I memorized every last detail. From the dreamcatcher tattoo on his shoulder blade to the feather that folded down over his deltoid, to the lighthouse and owl on his bicep, all the way to his sister's name scrolled along his muscular forearm. Every hard ridge and deep valley. Top to toe his body was a work of art. Smooth and sculpted.

I was happily perusing his abs, thinking his belly button was even sexy—as weird as that thought was—when Phoenix yanked his boxer briefs down his legs.

His erection sprang free and my gaze homed in.

"*Lawd*," I breathed.

Yes, I respired a word. Which was somewhere between panting and moaning. Hell, maybe I'd panted, moaned, and breathed at the same time. Maybe my thought wasn't audible at all. What I did know was Phoenix was a beast of a man and his cock was as big as the rest of him.

"Wren?"

"Yeah?"

"Only got one condom on me."

That was a damn shame.

"Okay."

"Look at me."

"Oh, I'm looking, honey."

I watched as his abs clenched and his erection bobbed as his chuckle filled my ears. It was a hard decision not to look up and see him smile, but I was transfixed on the bead of moisture leaking from the tip of his cock.

I wanted to lick it off, taste him, make him as crazy as he made me.

He used his foot to kick his pants up off the floor then bent to catch them midair. He was digging through his wallet and all the while my gaze remained on his cock. It lingered while I watched him roll the condom down his thick length. It stayed fastened there until I lost sight of it when his knee hit the bed. My legs automatically spread wider to accommodate his large frame. Phoenix dropped forward, but at the last second, he planted his hand on the mattress next to my shoulder.

"Wren?"

I attempted to drag my eyes to his, but I got sidetracked, stopping to admire his perfectly sized nipples, then paused again to take in his throat, then over his square jaw, until finally, I made it to my destination.

"Baby," he muttered with a smile.

I didn't understand what he found amusing.

"Yeah?"

"Christ, you're fucking gorgeous."

"So are you."

His smile grew when he asked, "You think you're gonna be able to hold out more than a few minutes?"

"Huh?"

"You damn near suffocated me." Unease crept in and his eyes narrowed. "That is not a complaint."

"Sounded like one."

"Baby, that was hot as fuck. I'd be pretty displeased if me going down on you *didn't* get you off. I plan on eating you every chance I get; it'd suck if you just laid there while I enjoyed myself. I like knowing all it takes is my tongue to get you to detonate. But as I said, I only got one condom, so you think you can hold out for more than a few minutes before you attack?"

"I didn't attack, and it'd been a long time."

"No shit?" I squinted my warning. Unfortunately, Phoenix didn't heed it when he continued, "It might've been my mouth, but it was you doing the work fucking my tongue."

"How about we stop right here?"

"Got a better plan—how about we see how fast I can get you wild?"

I liked his plan better.

I didn't tell him that.

I felt his hand working between us, then the head of his cock, and then in one hard thrust Phoenix filled me.

The air whooshed from my lungs, my back arched until only my shoulders were on the bed, and a long deep moan ripped from my throat.

"Oh my God."

Phoenix froze above me.

Totally and completely still, except for his eyes. They were roaming my face.

"You good?" he rumbled.

"No."

"No?"

No, I was absolutely not okay. I'd never been so full in my life. Never been stretched to the point of borderline pain.

"I need you to move."

He lowered himself to his elbow, giving me some of his weight. I knew he would feel great. I knew lying under him I would feel safe and protected.

I knew it.

And I was right.

"Wrap your legs around me."

I righted my back and shifted my legs until they were hooked around his hips.

When he still didn't move I lifted my hips and rocked into him.

"Hungry," he groaned.

Yes, I was hungry for his cock and if he didn't start moving and do that soon I would take over.

"Yes."

"No, baby, you're not hungry, you're fucking starved."

He pulled out and drove back in.

"Let's see about filling you up."

Yes, let's.

And that was what he did. He fucked me hard and fast and when I was seeing stars he backed off until my climax waned. He did this too many times. Driving deep, getting me close only to slow to a pace that would keep me *right* on the edge. He cupped my breast and toyed with my nipple, he pinched and twisted until I was gasping for air then he'd stop and gently glide his thumb over it. He bit and sucked along my shoulder until I was trembling then he'd slowly lick under my jaw. If he was driving deep, he was lightly grazing my nipple; if he was giving me slow, lazy glides with his cock he was biting my neck and pinching my nipple.

It made me crazy.

I could take no more.

"Phoenix," I groaned.

"Yeah, baby?"

"Stop teasing me."

He didn't stop. He continued with his torture until I snapped.

My hands roaming his back slid down to cup his firm ass. I unlocked my legs, planted my feet on the bed, and bucked my hips.

"I need..."

I got no more out. Phoenix hooked my right leg under his forearm and slammed home.

Yes. That was what I needed.

Another hard jolt. One more after that, then he paused mid-stroke and stared down at me.

"Starving."

"Yes," I readily agreed.

"No, not you. Me," he rumbled and slid in. "Can't get enough of you." He slowly slid out. "I can't get my fill." Another gentle glide. "You and me, baby, we're the same."

"Yes."

"The same but different."

I didn't understand what that meant but I didn't get a chance to ask.

Phoenix was done talking. His rhythm went straight to punishing and the orgasm that had been waiting in the background shot front and center.

I held my breath in preparation, but it lingered. I was so close, teetering but scared I was going to come apart at the seams.

"Let go," Phoenix grunted.

"Can't."

"Baby, let fucking go."

He sounded like he was straining. His ass muscles were flexing under my palms, his pelvis was slamming into mine, and my boobs were pressed tight against his chest. We were fully connected. Touching. His weight on me. His cock filling me.

Perfect.

Phoenix reached around, grabbed my wrist, twisted it, and threaded our fingers together before he pinned my hand above my head.

"Christ, baby, you gotta let go."

And that did it. Something about him holding my hand, anchoring me to him, threw me over—way over.

I came, screaming my orgasm.

Phoenix came, growling his.

But we finished with Phoenix's tongue in my mouth and me swallowing his groans.

It was...

Everything.

13

"Phoenix?"

All my life growing up I'd caught shit for my name. Not as much as Echo and River did, but enough that I wasn't particularly fond of it. But hearing Wren say it in a lazy, tired voice while she was sprawled naked over top of me was almost as good as hearing her scream it while her pussy pulsed around my cock until she sucked me dry.

When I came back into her room after disposing of the condom, I wasn't sure what I was expecting, but Wren naked on her back with her torn tee still on wasn't it. I figured she would've covered herself in some way. But she was exactly as I'd left her. That was until I crawled in next to her, then she rolled into me, rested her head on my chest, and used her arm and leg to pin me to the bed.

Now she was nuzzled in, my hand was cupping her bare ass, and I was wondering how much time we had before Griff was going to come home.

When she didn't continue, I prompted, "Yeah, baby?"

"I forgot what I was going to say."

I stared up at her ceiling and smiled.

"Tired?"

"I think I died twice."

"I think those are called orgasms."

"Oh, yeah, right. I had two really freaking great orgasms so yes, I'm tired."

I would venture to say she was understating her climaxes. The first one spilled into my mouth while she damn near ripped my hair out, and if the second one felt half as good as mine it was fucking phenomenal.

"Need to talk to you about something," I started, and I felt her body tense. "I need to know about Bill."

"Bill? What about him?"

She was no less stiff when I explained, "That scene at your house was intense. It rattled you and pissed off Griff. We haven't talked about him."

I felt a waft of warm air across my chest before she started to pull back. I tightened my arm around her and moved my hand from behind my head to her thigh so I could hold her where I wanted her.

"Don't pull away."

"I'm not pulling away. I just don't want to talk about this while I'm in bed naked with you."

"Why?"

"Because it's weird."

I had no idea if it was weird or not. I hadn't laid in bed with a woman and talked after sex since my high school girlfriend. I didn't get off and leave but I did get off and then get out of bed. Lying in bed with a woman holding her sent the wrong message.

"Nothing weird about it. I told you; you were safe with me. That includes naked in bed--no that means especially when you're naked in bed curled into me. You can tell me anything, anywhere, and you'll be safe to do it."

She blew out another breath. This time, the stiffness ebbed.

"Remember the letters that Griff found?"

"Yeah."

"I hadn't read them, but after Griff admitted he had I took the time to read them. There was nothing of importance in them, no apology to Griff, no words of regret. He doesn't ask me about Griff, how he's doing, what his new school is like—nothing. They're all about him and this money that he wants us to have. Bill has control over the account, and he wants me to get in contact with Bill to get the money turned over to me. Conor says the money's for Griff's education."

"Is the money clean?"

"I would assume so. Conor wasn't into shady deals, at least not that I knew about, and when he was being investigated for murder, I would think the detectives combed through his bank accounts and business records."

She was correct, the investigation would've included his financials.

"So why don't you want the money?"

She shrugged but didn't answer verbally. I stared at the ceiling prepared to wait her out. Just because I didn't have experience with after-sex cuddling didn't mean I wasn't well-versed in women. My sister had taught me a great many things about the tones and gestures women use. I knew when her tone pitched high, she was pissed, when it pitched low her feelings were hurt. When her hands went to her hips, she was getting ready to throw attitude. When she shrugged, she wasn't ready to talk. Unless any of the above had an "I'm fine" attached to it, then that meant all hell was about to break loose.

"May I ask you something personal?"

Fuck.

The familiar acid swirled in my gut, but I still pushed out, "Yeah."

"Griff talks to you about your dad?"

"Yeah."

"And you're okay with that? I mean, I could—"

"I'm more than fine with it. I want him to ask. I want him to understand that there's nothing he can't come to me about."

She nodded, then after a beat she whispered, "How can I hate him so much when half of him is in my son?"

The oxygen evacuated my lungs, leaving a trail of charred remains.

Jesus fuck.

Wren hadn't meant to land the blow, but her aim was true. There was the crux of all of my issues. I forced myself to stay still, not jump out of bed and run. I was good at that, good at running and hiding, but I wasn't good at staying and facing the shit I didn't want to face.

Echo had been right, I needed to stop lying to myself.

I had to own the truth or the lies I told myself would eat at my soul.

"Echo told me it was okay to love my father and hate the murderer. He said that to me the night I bailed on you and Griff. I left because Griff was right, I did understand what he was going through better than anyone and I'd let him down. I left because I didn't feel like I was good enough to be around him. I had a shit father, so what did I know about being a good role model to a teenager? I wasn't even off your street when I called Echo. He heard the pain in my voice and rushed to my apartment. I told him what happened, and he was pissed as fuck at me. He told me to fix it."

I stopped to take a breath and pulled her closer.

"Straight up, Wren, I wasn't sure. After that night, fucking up a second time, not doing right by Griff I thought both of you would be better off without me in your life. That's what I had to sort out. And part of the reason why I was able to do that is because Echo reminded me—my asshole father didn't raise me, Echo did. And he gave me the example I needed to do right by Griff. He also told me I needed to stop lying to myself. I've spent decades hating Lester, forgetting any sliver of good he had in him to hold on to that hate. You said something to Griff the other day and you were right to say it. You hate what he did, you hate the choices he made, but there has to be some good in him. He helped you make Griff and there is not one fucking thing about that boy that isn't special and right and perfect. Hate the murderer but it's okay to find the good in him."

I felt a drop of wetness hit my chest, then another, and another.

"Baby?"

Wren dipped her chin and hid her face.

I wasn't a fan of her hiding so I brushed the hair off her cheek and put gentle pressure under her chin until her head was tipped back and her tear-filled eyes met mine.

Good Christ, the woman was even beautiful when she cried.

"No hiding, baby, we're free of that."

"You're not gonna leave us."

I wasn't sure if that was a question or a statement, but I felt it imperative she unequivocally understood.

"No, I'm not gonna leave. I want to be clear, I understand with you comes Griff. I promise you I wouldn't be where I am with you right now if I wasn't positive that I was where I needed to be in my head to give Griff what he needs. Something else—what I'm building with Griffin is for Griff. That's between me and him and that has nothing to do with you or my feelings for you. Me being in this bed with you does not change me and Griff. Understand?"

Wren nodded.

"Good. Now I have one more question, then we're gonna circle back around and get to the part where you kiss all my aches and pains so I can kiss yours and we can be up and dressed before your son gets home from the movies."

"I thought you only had one condom."

"I did," I confirmed. Wren's brows pulled together. Her face went straight to perplexed. Jesus, I didn't want to know and I wasn't going to ask how shitty her sex life had been with her ex, but it was obvious. So instead, I told her, "Don't need a condom to make you come with my fingers, baby, and I've been waiting for what feels like forever to have your mouth on my cock so we're gonna do that, too."

"But we just...um..."

"Are you telling me you got your fill and now you're done?"

"No, but aren't you?"

"Wren, you're lying on me naked, your tits pressed against my chest and I'm semi-hard. And I'm only half hard because I'm trying to have a civilized conversation with my woman, and I think sporting a hard-on while talking about important shit would take the civilized out of that."

"Oh, I didn't think guys could..."

Fucking hell, this poor woman.

"Don't know about guys, but if you thought that we were done after one go, you're in for a treat."

She lifted her hand off my chest and let it fall back down with a slap.

"Don't make fun of me."

"Wren, baby, learn quick, I'm not making fun of you. I might tease you, but I'd never fucking make fun of you. I don't know who put it in your head that you letting go and enjoying sex wasn't hot but they were wrong. Or they didn't know what to do with you when you ignited. Lucky for you, you now got a man who not only knows what to do but enjoys the fuck out of it when you get rough."

My hand slid down to her ass crack, curled around, and I slid two fingers into her already wet pussy.

Following my lead Wren's hand glided down my chest, skimmed over my abs, and with a firm grip slowly stroked my cock.

"Tip your head back so I can kiss you."

Without delay, she did as I asked.

I'd had every intention of kissing her, but when she smiled, I was rendered useless.

"You're so fucking beautiful."

Her smile changed, it didn't widen so much as one side hitched up a little higher, and it went from sweet to sultry. Wren closed the distance, pressed a hard closed mouth kiss to my lips, moved to my jaw, then throat, and continued peppering kisses over my chest until she stopped at my nipple and swirled her tongue.

"Keep stroking, baby."

Her hand resumed stroking and her lips grazed down my abs not stopping until I felt her lips brush over the head of my cock.

"Up on your knees, baby, and ass facing me. I wanna play while I watch you suck me off."

I felt her pussy clench around my fingers right before they slid free.

Wren quickly got to her knees, bent forward, and without preamble slipped my cock into her mouth and with her fingers wrapped tight around the base of my shaft she got down to it. I could do nothing but lie there and enjoy it. Her mouth was goddamn bliss. It didn't take her long to find a rhythm that felt really fucking great but was really fucking bad for my control. And it wasn't long after that she had me ready to come.

"Ease up, baby, I'm ready."

Her tongue flattened against the underside of my cock, and she pulled up. I thought she was going to pop off but at the last second, she swirled her tongue around the tip before she slid back down. I fought the urge for as long as I could, but it was a losing battle. The woman gave good head —excellent, actually. But that was only part of it. She was into it and watching her suck me off as she moaned around my shaft was too fucking much.

"Baby, fair warning, pull off and finish me with your hand or you're getting a mouthful of come."

That was my second and final warning.

"Wren, baby, *fuck*."

Pleasure swept over me until I was afraid I was going to drown in it.

Wren slowed and it took me a moment to come back to the room. When the haze melted away, she came back into focus in time for me to watch her pull off and swallow one last time. That was hot as fuck, but the come dripping down her chin was so insanely hot my spent cock twitched. She used the back of her hand to wipe her mouth and she did it looking me dead in the eyes smiling.

Fuck yeah, she totally got off on sucking my cock.

"Proud of yourself?"

Her smile grew bigger, her beautiful eyes danced, and she nodded.

"You've got a big dick, Phoenix. I wasn't sure how that was gonna work. But I powered through it and brought it home. So, yeah, I'm pretty proud of myself."

I jolted in surprise right before I belted out a laugh.

∼

Wren and I were in the living room when Griff got home. We'd heard the car pull into the driveway and she picked her head up off my lap and straightened on the couch.

We'd discussed this after we'd cleaned up and gotten dressed. Griff needed to be slowly introduced to the idea of me and Wren being together. Not too much time, but enough that he'd be comfortable with the idea of me being with his mom.

So her sitting up and scooting a respectable distance was necessary.

Did I like the idea of finally finding a woman I wanted to explore something more with and having to take it at a snail's pace? Fuck no. But I was willing to put in the time and do what I needed to do to make sure Griff was where he needed to be.

"Hey! Good, you're still here," Griff chirped when he walked in.

Still here?

Wren's startled eyes came to me before she looked back at Griff and asked, "How was the movie?"

"Eh. It was okay. Not as good as the first but sequels never are."

I had no idea what movie he'd gone to but that didn't make his statement any less factual.

"Have you guys eaten? I'm starved."

Wren pinched her lips to hide her smile.

Yeah, this wasn't going to work. Griff was going to pick up on the change in his mom in two-point-five seconds.

"What's funny? Why are you smiling?"

And I was wrong. It had taken one-point-seven seconds.

"Nothing's funny. We haven't eaten. What are you hungry for?"

"Burgers?"

Wren jumped up off the couch like next week's winning lotto numbers were floating around her kitchen and would disappear at any moment so she needed to rush in there and jot them down.

"Phoenix, you want one?" She paused then reworded her question, "I mean, if you'd like to stay... you don't have to but if—"

"Wren," I cut off her babbling. "Yes, I'm staying and yes I'd like a burger, but with cheese."

"Sure."

Wren all but ran out of the living room. Griff's eyes bounced from me to his mom and then back to me.

"Why is she acting so weird?"

Fuck.

I didn't want to lie.

Taking it slow in front of him wasn't lying.

But being asked a question and not giving a straight answer was a damn lie.

"She finally tell you she loves you? Is that why she's being all giggly like a girl?"

Griff never failed to take me by surprise. Sometimes he was mature and articulate and other times he was still a goofy boy. And I never knew in any given situation which Griff I'd get.

"No, bud, she did not tell me she loves me."

His brows hit his hairline when he asked, "Did you tell her that you love her?"

Jesus.

"Nope. Neither of us professed any avowals of love while you were at the movies."

"Damn," he muttered under his breath.

And since I knew Wren let "damn" slide as far as cursing went, I didn't correct him.

"Can we go see the horses tomorrow?"

"Sure, but not until the afternoon. I'm playing basketball with Echo in the morning."

I saw it.

The kid couldn't hide it.

He'd yet to go play ball with me and I knew he wanted to. But after he'd told me he had no interest in playing, I told him if he changed his mind, he had to ask.

"Okay."

The disappointment was so thick I couldn't stop myself from giving the kid a little push.

"All you have to do is ask."

"What?"

"If you've changed your mind, you need to speak up."

Realization lit in his eyes. So did relief.

"Can I go with you to play ball?"

And just because he was a fourteen-year-old coming into his own he added a jerk of his chin at the end of his question.

Uncanny.

"Of course, you can. But you have to ask your mom and make sure it's okay with her."

"I better ask now, while she's in a giggly girl mood."

Griff went to the kitchen, and I relaxed back into the couch while I waited for him to come back and tell me Wren said yes. It was a given—no question she'd give that boy anything she could to make him happy.

It wasn't until that moment it hit me—Griff had asked if Wren had told me she loved me or if I had told her. There was no worry, no discomfort, no hostility. The kid not only liked the idea, but he was fully on board.

A moment after that it dawned on me that in the past the mere inkling a woman was starting to have feelings for me, I bolted. But with Wren, it was she who needed to catch up and fall for me, and I was staying to make sure that happened.

14

"I know you're seeing Phoenix," Griff said from behind me.

With my hand trembling, I curled my fingers around the bottle of coffee creamer and straightened, bringing the bottle out of the fridge.

How did he know?

Did he see Phoenix sneaking out?

Oh, God, I was thirty-four and my boyfriend has been sneaking in after my kid goes to sleep and then sneaking out at dawn.

Worse, it'd been going on two damn months, and it had been that long because I was too much of a chickenshit to talk to Griff.

And what made it even worse was that Phoenix was letting me have this and he was doing so because he cared about me and Griff, not because it was what he wanted. In the last two months, he'd bitched once. And that was only because it was late and he was pretend-leaving as Griff was going to bed, knowing that he was just going to go drive around the block a few times then come back. And even then, he didn't say anything, he'd just given me a scowl before he left.

He and Griff still hung out and did their thing. Sometimes if Phoenix had a shift, Shiloh, Luke, or Echo would pick him up from school and hang with him. Sometimes they took him out, or to see the horses, or Echo would take him to play ball. A few times Shiloh brought him home and just hung out at my house until I got home. Then there were times when he simply walked home from school, which I no longer minded. I had my happy, trustworthy, respectful boy back. I was no longer worried that in a fit of misplaced teenage boy rage he'd burn the house down—not that I thought he'd *really* do that, but I had not felt comfortable leaving Griff alone with his thoughts for the hours between when he got out of school and I got home from work.

So with all of that, Phoenix had been around a lot. He was at our house with us a lot. He stayed for dinner a lot. Actually, a lot meant almost every day. In the last eight weeks, I'd only slept alone a handful of nights and that was only because Phoenix had to work.

But we'd been careful.

Or at least I thought we had.

I set the bottle down next to my mug of coffee and faced my son, who was no longer a little boy.

Sneaking around was skirting the line of lying and I wouldn't even dip my toe over that line by asking why he thought that.

So the truth it was.

"Yes, I'm seeing Phoenix."

I'd had no expectations about what my son's reaction was but his lips twitching in amusement wouldn't have made my top ten guesses.

"I knew it," he semi-repeated. "So now that I know, does that mean he can stay for breakfast instead of leaving?"

Busted.

It took everything I had to hold myself together.

I felt like I was the teenager and Griff was the parent and I was on the verge of being grounded.

There was a knock on the front door before it opened and Phoenix walked in. That was what he did when he came over, he always knocked before he let himself in. I didn't know why he did it, maybe to announce his presence, but either I or Griff had to unlock the door ahead of time, so we always knew when he was coming over anyway.

"And maybe give him a key," Griff smoothly put in.

"Give who a key?" Phoenix scowled.

"You. It'll make coming over in the middle of the night easier."

At that, I lost my hold on cool. I wasn't in a full-on freakout but I was venturing that way.

"Come again?" Phoenix asked.

"How long have you known?" I snapped.

Griff shrugged and shook his head.

That was his go-to for when he didn't want to lie but he wasn't going to answer truthfully.

"Why didn't you say something sooner?"

"Why didn't you?" he threw back.

Damn.

This honesty shit sucked.

"First, because things had been rocky, and they were just smoothing out. Second, because I wanted time with Phoenix to make sure everything was going to work out before we told you. And the third reason is, some things in my life are private and I wasn't ready to discuss them with you."

Griff was nodding his head like he understood. Then he

looked at Phoenix and stood a little straighter. Something came over him and fear crept in. I'd seen that look a lot when Griff had taken his walk on the punk teenager side.

I braced.

"You're not gonna take off on my mom and hurt her, are you?"

Whoa. What?

Phoenix shifted to give Griff his full attention and when he answered his voice was firm but not in the parental tone I'd heard him use on Griff when he was jacking around and blowing off his chores. Just because the disrespect and general bad attitude had vanished didn't mean that Griff wasn't still a kid who occasionally needed to be corrected. This tone was different, man-to-man, respectful, humble.

"No, son, I'm not."

Griff studied Phoenix and Phoenix allowed this to go on for a while.

"I looked into it," Griff weirdly announced. "Conor's in prison so it would be easy. When you two get married, I want Phoenix to adopt me."

I was unclear what was happening to me. At that moment too many conflicting and extreme emotions swept through me. Grief that my boy had a father who was in prison. Elation he'd accepted Phoenix into our lives. Envious that at fourteen my son was brave enough to voice his needs. And extreme fear that it was far too early in my relationship with Phoenix to be talking about him adopting Griff.

I had yet to get a handle on all my feelings and decide on one when the vibe in the room turned electric. The air in the kitchen suddenly felt like it was lacking oxygen and it had gotten hard to breathe.

Everything changed.

Phoenix changed.

Griffin shifted from foot to foot, and I was worried he was preparing to flee.

Phoenix said nothing but I watched him clench and unclench his jaw.

Both my boys looked like they were locked in an emotional mortal combat.

One of them needed to say something.

Then finally Phoenix broke the silence.

"One day when you are a man, I will explain to you the fullness of what you saying that means to me. Until then I need you to understand something, and this is important, you listening?"

Griff nodded so Phoenix continued, "I love you. Full stop. I respect you and care about you. Full stop. I don't need a piece of paper to make you my son. Today, tomorrow, twenty years from now that is your choice. It's not mine. I don't get to decide how you feel about me or what you want to call me. You want that piece of paper, you want my last name, I will stop at nothing to get that for you, Griffin, as long as you understand that is not what makes me love you. That is not what makes us a family. You get that?"

"Yes," Griff choked out.

"Good. Now to go back to the earlier conversation. I take it we've been outed?"

"Yes," I answered around the emotion clogging my throat.

"Thank God," he groused. "I was getting tired of waking up at the butt-ass crack of dawn."

"Yeah, I noticed you've been leaving later and later," Griff teased.

Sweet mother of God, how long had Griff known?

"I know you saw me," Phoenix tossed back. "Pro tip—

when peeking out your curtains, don't open them in the middle, look out from the side and make sure the room is pitch black, or else the light shines through."

"You knew he saw you and you didn't tell me?"

"Baby, it was the first week and you were having a hard enough time keeping cool. The kid knew the night he got home from the movies and you jumped up like a schoolgirl—"

"Don't finish that, Phoenix Kent," I growled.

"I've known the whole time," Griff admitted.

"What?" I screeched. "Why didn't you talk to me?"

Griff did a one-arm shrug but put in, "You were happy and I didn't want you worrying about me."

The room fell silent.

I was busy having a mini freakout wondering if I was permanently scarred from realizing my son had known from day one his mom had a sleepover boyfriend and I wasn't sure that was something a fourteen-year-old should know.

And what if he...

"Wren?" Phoenix called.

"What?"

"Baby, you're thinking so hard over there the room's filling with smoke."

"Is someone gonna make breakfast? I'm starving."

"Yeah, you and Phoenix are. And while you're doing that, I'm going to take a shower and get ready. When you're finished cooking, find Phoenix a key."

I started to stomp out of the kitchen when Phoenix's arm shot out and hooked me around the waist waylaying my grand and dramatic exit.

When he had me pinned to his chest his mouth dropped

to my ear and he whispered, "You know I love you, too, right?"

No, I didn't know that. I knew he cared about me. I knew he liked me and I'd even go so far as saying he liked me a lot. I'd guessed he loved Griff but no, I had not known he loved me.

And right then I couldn't deal with the emotional overload of the morning.

"I don't know what to say," I whispered back, and Phoenix's body started shaking.

Was he laughing?

"You don't love me?"

"You know I do," I huffed.

"Then why don't you know what to say?"

"Because I've never been this happy."

Phoenix stopped shaking. Actually, he stopped moving altogether to the point he'd turned to stone.

"You've never been this happy?"

"Well, except for the day Griff was born."

"Fuck," he growled.

I knew that growl. I knew what it meant. I'd heard it nightly for the last two months. One could say I was having the best sex of my life, even if that sex was muffled by Phoenix's hand over my mouth or my favorite—his mouth over mine. I heard that growl when I did something he liked or said something sweet and that rumble always led to an orgasm. Unfortunately, that was not going to happen this time. But maybe later. No, *definitely* later.

"I love you, Phoenix."

This time I got the rumbled growl without the "fuck."

I pressed a chaste kiss to his lips, the first kiss my son had ever witnessed me giving a man and stepped out of Phoenix's arms.

My exit was no less grand when I made my way through the dining room to the hallway, but I didn't do it stomping, I did it floating.

∼

"Would you consider coming to work for Womens, Inc.?"

At Quinn's question, I pulled my gaze from Chelsea giving Griff a riding lesson on the back of her horse Rebel to the women around the table.

Phoenix, Luke, Matt, Brady, Trey, and Quinn's husband —hot guy firefighter Brice—were in the barn stacking hay in the loft, leaving me, Shiloh, Quinn, Hadley, and Addy sitting on the back porch.

"Are you talking to me?" I asked.

"Well, I wasn't asking Miss Badass SWAT Goddess over there. Though if I could convince her to quit the force and come work with us I think Echo would buy me a yacht and Phoenix and River would throw in a beach house."

"You're not wrong," Shiloh muttered.

"You want me to work there full time?" I asked.

"Yeah, we've been talking with Josie and she thinks we need to expand. The Hope Center will reopen in a few months so we'll be back in there full time. There's another center on the other side of Hollow Point. The facilities aren't as nice as the Hope Center. Actually, it's pretty run down. We want to take it over but we don't want to lose our original mission statement—women helping women. We have to keep that relevant. Sawyer can't do it alone. Lauren helps out a lot but she still works at TC. If she quit there'd be pandemonium. Addy, Hadley, and I can't do it. Hadley's going on maternity leave so she'll have time to devote to helping you get the new center going. Addy won't be too far behind her..."

As soon as the words left Quinn's mouth, Addy sucked in a breath. Quinn's gaze traveled to her sister and skewered her with a death glare.

"Don't act surprised. I know you didn't eat one too many Big Macs on your way over here and everyone knows that you don't have the twenty-four-hour flu. I'm so furious with you that I've decided that when I get pregnant, I'm naming my first child Hadley and my second will be Delaney and if I have a third I'm naming that one Hadley, too. And don't even *think* about naming my niece Quinn; it won't soften me up. I'm holding this grudge for eternity, and you know I can do it."

Addy looked properly chided. She also looked like she'd been struck, and I felt horrible for her. I'd gotten to know her a little over the last few months and she didn't have a mean bone in her body. Her secret was kept out of love. Though it was the most well-known secret I'd ever heard.

I didn't understand why Quinn would name her children after her sisters. It was cute but it would be damn confusing.

Apparently, this meant something big to Addy because the hurt wore off pretty damn quickly and she fired back.

"Fine," she huffed. "Hold your grudge. Be mad at me because I love you. See if I care."

"You care," Quinn hissed.

"Ignore them," Hadley told me. "Growing up, everyone always thought because Addy and I were twins that we'd fight the most. We didn't. It was Quinn and Addy or Quinn and Delaney. Are you seeing a common thread here? And now as grown-ass women, they sound like they're twelve."

When Hadley was finished two sets of squinted eyes

turned on her. I glanced at Shiloh who was watching the women, smiling.

"I don't know, sister, I grew up with three brothers. When they fought blood was shed then it was over. When they fought with me and I wanted them to give in and shut up, I just told them I was on my period and they ran."

"No. Did you really?"

"Hell yes, I did. Three brothers. They'd gang up on me but mention your period to a teenage boy and voila, you get what you want. The crazy part was I could use that excuse three or four times in one month and they'd believe it. I haven't asked but I'm pretty sure they still think a woman can have 'that time of the month' multiple times in one month. Try it, you can thank me later."

"Can we maybe get back to talking about what it would take to get Wren on board and finish the family drama later?" Hadley asked diplomatically.

"No, we cannot until I hear Addy say she's pregnant."

Once again the sisters locked eyes.

I didn't think Addy had it in her to face down her big sister.

I was right. Addy broke first.

"I'm pregnant," she whispered.

I held my breath and waited but it whooshed out when Quinn's chair scraped on the concrete and she stood and lifted her hands in the air while letting out a very loud whoop complete with jazz hands.

"My sister's having a baby!"

"She's a little crazy," Hadley stage-whispered.

As fast as Quinn stood, she switched up tactics, placed both hands on the table, and leaned in deep.

"I love you, little sister, but don't ever pull that shit again. I know why you did it, and I love you all the more for it. But you trying to protect my feelings means you deprived me of something special. You took that from all of us. That baby you're growing is *my* niece or nephew. He or she is a welcome addition to this family. Brice and I want a family, it's just taking us longer than we thought. But that doesn't mean we will love Hadley's spawn or your baby any less because we don't have our own. Understand?"

By the time Quinn was done I was blinking back tears.

"I get it and I'm sorry."

"Congratulations, Adalynn."

I watched as the first tear rolled down her cheek then I looked away.

Griff was happily chatting with Chelsea as she walked beside Rebel. Whatever my son said made Chelsea look up at him and smile.

My eyes drifted closed.

I wasn't stretching the truth when I told Phoenix that I'd never been this happy except for the day Griff was born. Never, not in my whole life, had I felt anything close to this kind of happiness.

Too bad I didn't know how quickly it could all be taken away.

15

The crunching of tires on gravel made me open my eyes. The other women at the table were looking at the driveway.

"Chelsea's gonna be pissed someone's coming down her driveway that fast," Hadley noted.

Yeah, the truck was going way too fast. Though whoever the driver was would be lucky to get Chelsea and not Matt. He didn't look like a man you wanted to cross, and I figured coming in hot and kicking up gravel he'd take as disrespect.

I glanced back to the pasture to double-check that my son was still in the fenced-in area.

The truck was coming closer and not slowing. I watched as Chelsea glanced over her shoulder, then suddenly she was jogging next to Rebel and pulling the halter. Not to the barn but to the gate that led out into a big open field.

What the hell?

"Get in the house," Shiloh barked.

Quinn, Hadley, and Addy silently got up and did as Shiloh had instructed.

"Griff—"

"Matthew!" Chelsea shouted.

I watched as she climbed the first rung of the fence and hoisted herself behind Griff on Rebel's back. Once up, she leaned to the side, unlocked the gate, and kicked it open with a booted foot.

Rebel charged through the gate, and they were off.

Phoenix, Matt, Luke, Trey, and Brice came running out of the barn.

Then everything happened all at once and it happened so quickly that there was nothing anyone could've done differently to avoid the tragedy that day brought.

The pickup truck skidded to a stop. The door opened and a gunshot blasted.

I jumped in surprise, then I screamed.

I heard more gunfire erupt—lots and lots of gunfire roaring over my screams.

I screamed so loudly and for so long my throat burned. But it was my heart that shattered.

I felt Shiloh's hands on me, grabbing my shirt, yanking me back. I heard the material tear. A fitting sound seeing as my heart had been torn from my chest.

It was now in the dirt next to Phoenix's prone body.

Brice was on his knees on Phoenix's right side, Luke was on his left, and when I made it across the yard, Matt and Trey were near the pickup.

I was almost to Phoenix when I slipped on gravel, stumbled, and went down. I muffled my cry of pain the best I could and crawled the last few feet to Phoenix. The first thing I noticed was Brice's hands were covered in blood. The next thing I noticed was that Luke's knees were also covered in blood. The last was that Phoenix's eyes were open.

I lowered my face to his and cupped his jaw.

"Hey."

"Griff?"

"Chelsea's got 'em."

"Don't let him see."

Shattered.

"Okay, honey."

I was jostled when Shiloh plopped down next to me, wrapped one arm around me, and reached for her brother's hand.

"Sunny—"

"Don't, brother. Ambo's on the way. You're gonna be fine."

"You know what I want—"

"Stop, brother. You're gonna be fine."

Phoenix's eyelids started to drift shut.

"No, honey, keep them open." I shook his face and demanded, "Look at me, Phoenix."

He slowly dragged his lids halfway open.

"Love you, Wren. Love Griff."

His eyes closed and so did mine.

I felt Shiloh's body buck. I heard her sob but after that, I heard nothing. I felt nothing. I was completely and totally numb.

The yard filled with flashing lights as police and EMTs flooded in.

I sat on my ass and watched them put Phoenix on a stretcher and load him into the back of an ambulance. Someone hoisted me to my feet, and I never took my eyes off Phoenix. I was lifted into a pair of strong arms, and I didn't protest that either.

"Griffin?"

"Quinn has him," Echo told me.

He carried me to the ambulance and climbed in. He sat down and kept me on his lap and I stared at Phoenix. The

EMTs worked on Phoenix, and I watched. One of them cut his bloody shirt open as the other one was starting an IV and I silently watched.

On the ride to the hospital, I was grateful Echo didn't speak. He didn't spew useless platitudes. He didn't promise me Phoenix would be okay. He didn't tell me he was sorry that the happiest day of my life had now turned into my worst.

Then the back doors to the ambulance opened to a flurry of commotion. The stretcher was pulled out and the EMTs jumped out behind it. I saw lips moving but heard nothing. Echo stood, adjusted me in his arms, and followed the stretcher. I kept my eyes on Phoenix until two doors swung closed and he was gone. I dropped my head to Echo's shoulder and burrowed in.

He still said nothing.

∼

Echo, Shiloh, Luke, me, and Griff were huddled together in the back corner of the waiting room. Trey and Brady stood guard not letting any of the many well-wishers by. The whole floor of the hospital was wall-to-wall police officers. One of their own had been shot. It didn't matter if it wasn't in the line of duty. They were there to pay their respects, not only to Phoenix but also to Shiloh and Echo.

The door opened and Quinn pushed in holding a white paper bag. She slowly approached and knelt down in front of Griff.

"I brought you a sandwich and some chips."

"Thanks, Quinn."

Griffin politely took the bag. Quinn reached up, cupped his cheek, and gave him a sad smile.

She stood and asked, "My dad's on his way and wanted to know if any of you needed anything?"

Echo spoke for the family when he declined.

We went back to sitting in silence. Shiloh leaned heavily into Luke, his arm around her holding her close. I had my head resting on Echo's shoulder, Griff was on his other side, and Echo's arm was around him.

And there we sat and waited.

I felt less than nothing.

"I think it's time to call River," Shiloh whispered.

"Not yet."

I closed my eyes in an effort to block out the conversation.

"Echo—"

"Not yet, Sunny."

"He's going to be fine," Griff announced.

"He is," Echo agreed, and I prayed that it wasn't a lie.

"I'm telling you he's gonna be fine," Griff said loudly.

I picked my head up off Echo's shoulder and looked at my boy.

So much fear shone in his eyes if my heart wasn't already shattered that would've done it.

"Griff—"

"He has to be okay!" he yelled.

"Hey," Echo called out softly, gently. He plucked Griff out of his chair like he was a toddler and stood my son on his feet in front of him.

"He has to be okay," Griff whispered. "I didn't get to tell him I love him."

"Bud, he knows you love him."

"I didn't tell him. He told me he loved me, and I didn't say it back. He has to be okay. I have to tell him."

That cut through the fog. I felt that. I felt my son's pain

so acutely my elbows went to my knees and my head dropped forward.

"Kent?"

"Here," Echo called back.

I couldn't move. I couldn't look. With my eyes wrenched closed, I blindly reached for Echo. His fingers curled around my hand, and I held on as tightly as I could.

"Phoenix is out of surgery."

I was sure more was said but I couldn't hear anything over whooshing in my ears.

He was out of surgery.

"When can we see him?" Shiloh asked.

"He's not awake yet, so one visitor for now."

"Wren."

I kept my head bowed and mumbled, "Huh?"

"Go on back."

"I don't think I can make it back there alone," I admitted.

"I'll take you."

Echo pulled me to my feet, kept his arm around me, and reached for Griff.

"My nephew goes, too," he told the doctor.

Seeing as Echo was six-foot-five and a wall of muscle, the doctor didn't quibble.

With Echo all but propping me up and my son holding my hand I zombie-walked down the hall. The crush of police officers parted to make room as we passed. The doctor stopped at a locked door, waved the badge around his neck over the sensor, and the door slowly swung open.

"You got her?" Echo asked Griff.

"Yeah."

"Good man," he muttered.

Echo kissed the top of my head and turned. But before he stepped away, I grabbed his arm.

"Thank you."

"Trust me, Wren, this is what he'd want."

"No, Echo. Thank you."

"He'd want that, too."

"Echo, *thank you*."

I watched his throat bob and he mumbled, "You're welcome."

I let go of Echo and Griff gave my hand an impatient tug.

Phoenix's room was at the very end of a very long hallway.

"You can wash your hands here." The doctor pointed to a small sink basin.

I heard the water turn on, but I kept my eyes locked on the man lying in the hospital bed on the other side of the glass door. He looked much too big for the tiny bed.

"Mom."

I shuffled to the sink, washed my hands, pulled some paper towels out of the dispenser, and did a half-ass job of drying them.

"Ready," Griff announced.

We followed the doctor in. He went right to the monitor and turned down the volume so it wasn't blaring, but high enough that I could still hear the steady rhythm of Phoenix's heart.

"Can I touch him?" Griff asked.

"Sure you can. Just be careful not to pull out the IV. I'll give you two a few minutes."

Just like the last time I saw him; his eyes were closed.

Pain bloomed in my chest.

I concentrated on the beat of his heart.

Griff gently picked up Phoenix's hand and that hurt, too.

"I didn't get to tell you, so I'm telling you now. I think you can hear me but if you can't I'll tell you again later. I love you, Phoenix."

That didn't hurt—that burned.

Open your eyes, I screamed in my head.

Phoenix didn't move, he didn't twitch, he didn't do anything. He just lay there.

I concentrated on the beat of his heart.

"Come on, Mom, talk to Phoenix."

I walked around to the side of the bed Griff was on and he scooted over to give me room. I looked down at a sleeping Phoenix Kent. He was no less beautiful than he always looked. Though he wasn't really sleeping, he was unconscious.

I almost lost him.

We almost lost him.

I felt it start. Everything I'd been holding back, everything I didn't want to feel came rushing back in a tidal wave of excruciating agony.

I leaned over Phoenix and dropped my forehead to his, careful not to dislodge his oxygen, and let my tears flow.

"We need you to wake up, Phoenix. You have to wake up and come back to us. Please, honey, wake up soon."

Griff's arms wrapped around my middle. His head rested on my back and we stood there together leaning over our shield. The man who'd brought us back to life. The man who was broken but still managed to piece us back together.

"Rest, baby, we'll be waiting for you."

All too soon I heard the doctor clear his throat.

This time when I walked down the hall, I heard every beep coming from the other rooms as we passed. I heard the door slide open. I heard voices and bits and pieces of conversations. I smelled the scent of disinfectant. I felt the ache down the left side of my body from my fall. I felt my son's warm hand in mine.

I also felt fear.

Fear that he wouldn't wake up and fear that he would. That he'd go to work, and he'd put himself in danger, and one day Griff and I would be right back here.

Echo, Shiloh, and Luke met us at the waiting room door.

"How's he look?" Shiloh asked.

"Too big for that little bed," Griff voiced my earlier thought.

"One of the many curses of being tall."

"He looks good," I answered. "His heart rate's steady and strong. His color looks good. He just looks like Phoenix."

Shiloh relaxed into Luke.

"Sunny and Luke are gonna stay here," Echo said. "I'm gonna take you and Griff home and bring you back in the morning."

"You don't—"

"I'm staying with you and Griff," he cut me off.

I wanted to stay and wait for Phoenix to wake up, but I didn't want Griff sleeping in a waiting room.

"I promise I'll call you if anything changes."

"Thanks, Shiloh."

Hugs were passed out then we were on our way.

The ride back to my house was much like the ride in the ambulance—silent.

Each of us lost in our own thoughts.

Mine were morbid and getting worse by the mile.

By the time Echo pulled into my driveway I was ready to come out of my skin. The front door had barely closed when Griff launched in.

"Phoenix is coming home with us, right?"

"I'm sure he'll have to stay in the hospital for a few days but yes, he'll be coming home."

"No." Griff shook his head. "Home with *us*. He'll need help when he gets out of the hospital. He'll be here, right?"

"Of course, he will be."

"Okay, good."

There was something worrisome about Griff's tone. It was borderline desperate.

"Griffin, today was…" I trailed off, trying to come up with the right word, but all my tired brain could come up with was, "Rough." Understatement. "I think we should talk about it."

Griff's eyes darted to Echo then back to me.

"I was scared," Griff admitted and pinched his lips.

"So was I."

"I thought… I thought…"

"What'd you think?"

"I thought he was going to die."

I was not ready for my teenage son to dash across the room and throw himself at me. Thank God, Echo was there to catch me before we went down. I wrapped my arms around Griff and Echo wrapped his around both of us. And in my man's brother's arms, my son and I finally let go.

Echo stood strong, holding us while the pain and fear of the day leaked out of us.

Standing there, I finally understood why Phoenix was who he was. I understood how he'd become the man he became. It wasn't because of any slivers of good that a man named Lester had. It was because Echo Kent had become a father at a very young age and gave Phoenix all the good he had inside of him. Echo taught him how to be the shield.

That gave me hope for Griffin.

After I tucked Griff into bed—something I hadn't done

in years—I made my way back into my living room and found Echo on the couch watching TV. I was dog-ass tired and emotionally drained, and I knew he had to be feeling it just the same as me.

"Why don't you sleep in my bed?" I asked as I sat next to him.

"I'll be fine out here. But you should get some rest."

"Has anyone ever told you that you're stubborn?"

"Only about seven million ninety-five times."

"Let me guess, your siblings are the majority of those."

"Yes, but only because they're all a pain in my ass."

I scooched back into the corner and bent my knees until my heels were resting on the edge of the cushion.

"Who takes care of you?"

"Come again?"

"You take care of all of them, it's my understanding you always have. So, who takes care of you?"

Echo's gigantic frame locked, and his piercing blue eyes sparked. Everything about him screamed to stay back. All he was missing was a flashing red sign on his head.

"I take care of me."

"And them."

"You going somewhere with this, Wren?"

If for the last ten hours this beast of a man hadn't taken care of me, been gentle with me, gentle with my boy, the vibes rolling off him would've scared me to death. But not now, not after he picked me up and carried me, then held me and gave me every bit of strength I needed to breathe.

"It's exhausting, isn't it? Having to pick up the pieces that other people break."

"Wren—"

I talked over him. "From as far back as I could remember, I've been cleaning up other people's messes. My dad would go out, get drunk, cheat on my mom, create a mess and not care. My mom would fight with Dad, scream, holler, spew more selfishness and not care. Their marriage was a mess, their personal lives a mess. But they didn't care. Then Conor did whatever Conor wanted to do and didn't care about anything or anyone but himself. More mess to clean up. He sure wasn't thinking about Griffin or me for that matter when he committed murder. Left his son without a father, more mess I have to clean up. He goes to jail, the whole city's talking about it, more mess for me. But this time, it's important. This time I can't fuck it up. So, to answer your question, I'm going nowhere with this. You've got help now, Echo. I told you about my parents and about my ex, so you'll understand that I'm an old hat at this. It's exhausting being everything for everyone. It's tiring cleaning up after everyone."

"Family sticks together," he told me.

"Absolutely."

"When it's family it's not a burden. You do what you have to do."

"Absolutely, but it doesn't make it any less exhausting. You've been in my shoes. You were a single parent. However, I've never been in yours. Your kids are grown, I'm still raising mine."

Echo jerked back and he tilted his head.

"Phoenix might be your brother, but he's also your son. I know what I was feeling when I was sitting in the dirt next to Phoenix. And I know you were feeling the same multiplied by a hundred, yet you took care of me. It was automatic for you. It's who you are. So, Echo, again— who helps you carry the load?"

He'd dialed up the laser beams and I wondered how many people cowed when he turned his scowl their way.

That made me wonder what kind of woman it would take to withstand his menacing stare.

"What exactly are you trying to get at?"

Oh, shit. Maybe I'd pushed too far.

Echo's growly voice was far, far different from Phoenix's. For one, Phoenix's was rumbly and sexy. Echo's was more like a roar and scary.

"Today fucking sucked," he said.

"Yeah, it did."

"I was goddamned terrified."

Finally.

"So was I."

"My fucking brother was bleeding out, my sister was breaking down, I was so goddamn fucking scared that we were gonna lose him and there'd be nothing I could do to fix that. It has always been the four of us, our family doesn't work without one of us. Christ." Echo's hand came up, they drove into his hair, and he yanked. "*Christ.*"

"I went numb," I whispered. "Totally numb. I felt nothing. When his eyes closed, I thought that was it, he was gone, and I didn't know what we were going to do without him."

"Christ. That crazy old fucking bastard."

He was talking about Milo. The very dead Milo.

"If Chelsea hadn't taken off with Griff it could've—"

"Don't do that," he cut me off.

"But then—"

"Wren! Do not fucking do that. You know my brother; he would rather die than have Griff harmed. My whole world is my brothers and my sister and I'm telling you, I'm glad that Chelsea took Griff and took off. Because you're right. That crazy motherfucker went there pissed because Chelsea took his horses. Do not mistake that; no one blames her, she did the right thing. But he was gunning for her and if she was there, she and Griff would've likely been hit."

We both fell silent. Echo leaned back on my couch, which was big and comfy, but with him sitting on it, it looked small.

With his eyes trained on the TV, he said, "Thank you."

"It's what Phoenix would want."

I heard him chuckle before he repeated, "Thank you, Wren."

"It's what family does, Echo."

"Has my brother ever told you you're a pain in the ass?"

I didn't need to think about it before I answered, "Nope."

There was another stretch of silence, this one longer, when Echo muttered, "Welcome to the family."

I smiled at the TV.

"Thanks, big brother."

After that, I fell asleep tucked into the corner of my couch.

16

"You're not supposed to be out of bed."

I swear to God, the woman had the hearing of a dog. My feet had barely hit the carpet.

"Has anyone ever told you you're a pain in the ass?" I smiled.

"Yes, your brother. Now, why are you out of bed?"

"I need to piss. You wanna help me, Nurse Wren?" I asked, only half joking.

"I think you can manage on your own."

She was right, I could.

"But it'd be more fun if you helped."

Wren crossed her arms over her chest and leaned her hip against the dresser.

"And what exactly is it you need help with?"

She was having a hard time keeping a straight face. It was good to see her smile. The morning I woke up in the hospital she certainly wasn't smiling. By that afternoon she was lying in my bed on my good side bawling her eyes out. It had taken me almost an hour to calm her down. I was not pleased my woman was sobbing but I was pleased I was alive to hold her.

When that crazy bastard got out of his truck and I saw the gun I thought I was as good as dead at that range. Thank fuck his aim sucked. I'd take a gutshot over one to the head any day of the week. Though, preferably I'd never take another to the gut or anywhere else.

"Got time for a sponge bath?"

"I got nothing but time," she reminded me.

Wren had taken two weeks off of work to take care of me. The first week I was home I did nothing but sleep but I was feeling better, and Griff was at school.

"In that case, a sponge bath with a double happy ending?"

"You have a bullet wound—"

"Yeah, but I didn't take a bullet to my cock."

Jesus.

That thought made me shudder.

"I don't think—"

"I'm not asking you to ride my cock. I'd settle for my face."

"That's not happening."

I was gauging my chances of talking her around when she asked, "Are you pouting?"

"Pouting? I'm a grown man, I don't pout."

"It sure looks like you were."

"Well, I wasn't."

"Then what were you thinking about?"

She adjusted her arms which brought my attention to her chest.

"C'mere, baby, and I'll show you what I was thinking."

Wren pushed away from the dresser and strutted her sexy ass across the room.

When she stopped close, I reached for the hem of her shirt and yanked it up. Her arms went up, and as soon as it was clear I tossed it on the floor. Wren's gaze dropped to her tee, then she looked back at me.

I was a lucky motherfucker.

"You know, Griff told me about the first time he went to your apartment that it was filthy."

"Yep. Total shithole," I agreed and pushed my sweats down my hips.

When they pooled around my ankles and I kicked them to the side, Wren glanced down at those, too.

"Griff said you didn't even know if you owned a vacuum."

The kid totally ratted me out.

"He's telling the truth," I admitted and undid her jeans.

Unfortunately, I couldn't bend down, so they were stuck mid-thigh.

"Take those off, baby."

Wren wiggled out of her jeans.

"Am I going to be cleaning up after you, too?"

My hand shot out, tagged her around the back of the neck, and brought her face close to mine.

"If I promise not to leave my dirty laundry on the bedroom floor, will you please sit on my face so I can eat you?"

Her lips twisted, then one side hitched up.

"Nope."

"What if I throw in picking up my wet towels and doing dishes three nights a week?"

"Add in vacuuming once a week and sweeping the kitchen once a week and you have a deal."

"Done."

Wren smiled, and for the first time since I'd been shot

the knot in my chest loosened. My hand skimmed the top of her panties before I pushed inside. My middle finger skimmed over her clit and her hips jerked.

"Bra off."

She reached around and unclasped her bra. I had her nipple in my mouth before her bra hit the floor. After I finished licking that one to a hard peak, I pulled back to move to the other side, grateful she was the perfect height. Before I pulled the other one into my mouth I asked, "What chores do I need to do to get you to suck me off?"

I circled her clit and flicked my tongue over her nipple, giving her nowhere near enough friction to get her off. My girl liked it rough, but I liked to tease her to the edge until she was mindless.

"None."

"None?"

I was smiling when I leaned forward and kissed her. My fingers slid through her wetness and I pushed two inside. Wren moaned against my tongue and my cock reminded me it had been too fucking long since I'd tasted her mouth. I broke the kiss and smiled when she groaned.

"Panties off."

I very carefully lowered myself to the bed, and I did this under the watchful gaze of Nurse Wren. One fraction of a wince and I knew she'd call the whole thing off.

"See, I'm fine."

"Uh-huh," she mumbled and stepped out of her panties.

I made quick work of getting situated.

"Hop on, baby."

She didn't hop on. She stood at the side of the bed and stared down at me.

"I love you, Phoenix."

I would never tire of hearing her say that to me.

"I love you, too, baby."

She continued to stare at me. Not my bandage, which I caught her doing a lot, but at me.

"You know, the first time I saw you I was taken aback by how good looking you are. Then I watched you with Griff in the gym and my heart literally hurt because I didn't think he'd ever have that in his life in a permanent way. Then you saved his life and all I could think was we'd found our hero, but he'd never be ours. And then that night you made dinner and were helping Griff with his homework, I watched you while thinking that was the most beautiful thing I'd ever seen but it wasn't for me to keep. And when I thought we lost you my heart shattered into a million pieces. There will never be another man for me. If I lost you, I would spend the rest of my life alone. I would live on the memories. The beauty you've given me."

Jesus fuck.

"Baby, come here."

"I need you to know that, Phoenix. Griff and I, we wouldn't go on."

"Wren. Come. Here."

She finally crawled into bed—carefully, gently, timidly. I would be so fucking happy when I was healed up. My girl was not careful, gentle, or timid with sex.

She was sitting ass-to-calves on the bed next to my hip.

"Remember that first morning when I showed up at your house?"

"Yeah."

"And before I left I told you I needed to stay away from you because if you pushed, I'd cave."

Wren's chin tipped down and she nodded.

"I remember all of it. Why?"

"That wasn't me warning you off, baby, that was me

begging you to fix me. I didn't have the first clue how to win a woman like you, but fuck did I need you."

"Phoenix," she whispered.

"Love it when you whisper my name, baby, but I wanna hear you scream it."

"I don't..."

She trailed off because my girl couldn't lie even when she was joking.

"Hurry up, Nurse Wren, I'm hungry."

Wren scooted up to my shoulders, swung her leg over, and glanced down at me.

"Dr. Wren."

"Yes, ma'am, Dr. Wren," I said around a smile.

I grabbed two handfuls of ass and my girl commenced riding my face. It took less than five minutes before she ignited and was grinding her pussy on my mouth, and I was courting sweet suffocation.

∽

"I DON'T THINK this is the proper technique for a sponge bath," I tsked.

"No? This is how Dr. Drake Ramoray taught me how to do it."

Wren circled the head of my cock with her tongue.

"Who?" I growled.

Wren's answer was to giggle around my cock.

She added a good amount of suction and twisted her hand around the base.

"Good Christ, your mouth is good."

When she got to the tip and pulled off she asked, "Was that the proper technique?"

I narrowed my eyes and shook my head. "I don't know

who this Dr. Ramoray is, Wren, but I'm feeling the need to track him down and kick his ass."

She kissed the underside of my shaft and shook her head. "Who knew my man was so jealous?"

She sucked the head back in her mouth but only bobbed on the first few inches.

My abs clenched and I growled to cover the pain that caused.

"Baby, *please* stop fucking around and suck my cock."

I watched the corner of her mouth hitch up and I knew if she didn't have a mouthful of cock she'd be smiling.

∽

WREN WAS SITTING NEXT to me back against the headboard. Griff was sitting on the corner of the bed cross-legged, and we were being tortured. That was, Griff and me. Wren was busting a gut laughing.

Since I'd come home from the hospital this had become our nightly routine. TV watching in our bed. This was because I couldn't get comfortable on the couch and neither Wren nor Griff wanted to leave me in the bedroom alone.

"Can you believe Lisa—"

"Wren, I love you, baby. From the bottom of my soul. But it's bad enough you're forcing me and Griff to watch this shit. We do not need a play-by-play. We're watching. Our brain cells are actually dying but we're watching."

"I'm thinking of moving out," Griff announced, and Wren's head swung his way. "I'm thinking Tibet. I bet they don't show this crap on TV in Tibet."

"I think I might join you," I muttered.

Wren tossed a handful of popcorn into her mouth and went back to her program.

"You boys have fun."

After a few minutes of watching some actress who used to be on *Melrose Place* yell at another woman, Griff looked at his mom.

"You know it takes the fun out of it if you don't get all huffy."

"Yep," Wren answered around another handful of popcorn.

Griff looked at me and shook his head. I shrugged, then we both looked back at the TV.

Sometime into the third episode, it hit me how Echo had it right all along. Even as a young man he understood what was important. All the nights me and my siblings would bitch because Echo would make us all sit in the living room and watch TV together instead of being in our rooms doing what we wanted to do.

It wasn't about what was on the TV screen. It was about sitting in the same room with your people. It was about spending time with them. Seeing them, not just glancing up from what you were doing and only half paying attention.

It was about the man who had become my father when he was still a boy teaching me what was important so I could one day pass it down to my boy.

"Will you please pass me the popcorn?" Griff asked.

Wren handed off the bowl, turned sideways, and rested her head on my thigh. Griff munched away. And I lay there with two of the most important people in the world and watched really bad TV.

But I did it smiling.

17

Echo Kent

"Thanks for picking me up," Griff said from the passenger seat.

"Anytime. Besides, I'm headed to your house anyway."

"Did Phoenix tell you that my mom said I could keep Dasher?"

"Good news, bud."

Like there was ever a doubt Wren would tell her boy he couldn't have one of the horses he helped rescue.

"Yeah. Sucks that Simon and King can't stay but Chels has her hands full with Rebel and Trigger and running "the bar" even with me going over there to help."

The kid used air quotes around "the bar" and I couldn't hold back my laughter. I hadn't been there, but the way Phoenix told the story Wren about had a heart attack when she got to Matt's house to pick up Griff and he was wearing one of Matt's Balls Deep shirts instead of his school shirt while painting the side of the barn. Griff hadn't noticed what the t-shirt said until his mom yelled at Phoenix for letting him wear it. The kid was fourteen—he knew what that meant so now when he calls it the bar he uses air quotes.

"Yeah, Chelsea's pretty busy."

I wasn't even out of the school parking lot yet when Griff asked, "May I ask you something?"

Born from years of practice, I kept my body loose and my tone even when I answered, "Sure, whatcha got?"

I really wanted to say fuck no. But this was Griff, and the kid was my nephew even if his mom and my brother hadn't made it official.

"Did Phoenix tell you that Conor set money aside for college for me?"

Shit.

"Yeah. He told me."

"Do you think I should take it?"

And there it was, the question I was afraid he'd ask. At first, Wren was completely against accepting any money from her ex. But since then, she'd softened to the idea. Phoenix didn't care one way or another. If Wren didn't take the money, Phoenix would back her and the same went if she took the money.

"What do you think you should do?"

"I don't want anything from him."

Yep, I figured that would be his answer. Just like my brother, the boy was holding on to anger instead of ridding himself of the burden.

"Education's important. It's also expensive. You're coming up on high school and in a few years, you'll have to start thinking about what you want to do after you graduate. That money might be a big help."

Griff fell silent and I waited until I stopped at a red light to glance over at him. "What're you thinking about?"

"You'll think it's stupid."

"Bud, I will never think anything you're thinking about or asking about is stupid."

"I think the guy's family who Conor killed should have it. He had kids. I think they need it."

Likely Conor's estate had paid restitution to the family. The money set aside for Griffin's college was probably in an account that couldn't be seized.

"Griff, that's far from stupid. That's kind and generous. Have you talked to your mom and Phoenix about it?"

"No. I wanted to ask you first."

I'd officially become a guardian at twenty-one. But long before that, I was already raising my siblings. That was damn near half my life being a parent. But Shiloh, Phoenix, and River stopped needing me in any real way a long time ago. I never thought I'd miss arguing about homework and cleaning the house, but it was far better than living alone in a spotless house. Griff had Phoenix, but it felt good to have the kid around, feeling needed again.

"Talk to your mom about it, tell her what you're thinking, then maybe wait awhile until you make a decision."

"Yeah. Okay. That sounds good."

My phone rang and one glance at the dash display made my jaw clench.

"Who's Jaclyn?" Griff inquired.

The woman who I fell in love with over a weekend then lost because I was a jackass.

"No one."

"Then why are you grinding your teeth?"

So, maybe I was wrong. Living in a quiet, clean house with no kids around was the way to go. I was too fucking old to be interrogated by a teenager. Been there, done that.

I ignored Griff's question and the call and made my turn onto Phoenix's street.

"You grunt just like Phoenix," he noted.

"No, Phoenix grunts like me."

Griff shifted in his seat and stared at me.

"Is there a difference?"

"Yes. I'm older. So Phoenix is copying me with the grunting."

"Okay," Griff muttered and went back to looking out the window.

My phone stopped ringing and my jaw relaxed.

I pulled into the driveway and shut my car down. But instead of hopping out of the car like he normally did when I brought him home, he sat there. I knew the kid's brain was working overtime. I figured he was about to call me out on Jackie when he veered way off track and asked, "You raised Phoenix, right?"

Not knowing where the conversation was leading, I warily answered, "I did."

Griff's face broke out into a wide shit-eating grin.

"So does that mean I should call you Uncle Echo or Grandpa Echo?"

I grunted.

The little shit's smile turned smug.

Echo Kent has always been the rock for his family. What they don't know is just how fractured he really is. Can a woman who is equally scarred help heal his past, or will Echo continue to hide behind duty and family obligation?

Fractured is up next

ALSO BY RILEY EDWARDS

Riley Edwards

www.RileyEdwardsRomance.com

Takeback

Dangerous Love

Dangerous Rescue

Dangerous Games

Dangerous Encounter

Dangerous Mind

Gemini Group

Nixon's Promise

Jameson's Salvation

Weston's Treasure

Alec's Dream

Chasin's Surrender

Holden's Resurrection

Jonny's Redemption

Red Team - Susan Stoker Universe

Nightstalker

Protecting Olivia

Redeeming Violet

Recovering Ivy

Rescuing Erin

The Gold Team - Susan Stoker Universe

Brooks

Thaddeus

Kyle

Maximus

Declan

Blue Team - Susan Stoker Universe

Owen

Gabe

Myles

Kevin

Cooper

Garrett

The 707 Freedom Series

Free

Freeing Jasper

Finally Free

Freedom

The Next Generation (707 spinoff)

Saving Meadow

Chasing Honor

Finding Mercy

Claiming Tuesday

Adoring Delaney

Keeping Quinn

Taking Liberty

Triple Canopy

Damaged

Flawed

Imperfect

Tarnished

Tainted

Conquered

Shattered

The Collective

Unbroken

Trust

Standalones

Romancing Rayne

Falling for the Delta Co-written with Susan Stoker

AUDIO

Are you an Audio Fan?

Check out Riley's titles in Audio on Audible and iTunes

Gemini Group

Narrated by: Joe Arden and Erin Mallon

Red Team

Narrated by: Jason Clarke and Carly Robins

Gold Team

Narrated by: Lee Samuels and Maxine Mitchell

The 707 Series

Narrated by: Troy Duran and C. J. Bloom

More audio coming soon!

BE A REBEL

Riley Edwards is a USA Today and WSJ bestselling author, wife, and military mom. Riley was born and raised in Los Angeles but now resides on the east coast with her fantastic husband and children.

Riley writes heart-stopping romance with sexy alpha heroes and even stronger heroines. Riley's favorite genres to write are romantic suspense and military romance.

Don't forget to sign up for Riley's newsletter and never miss another release, sale, or exclusive bonus material.

Rebels Newsletter

Facebook Fan Group

www.rileyedwardsromance.com

facebook.com/Novelist.Riley.Edwards
instagram.com/rileyedwardsromance
bookbub.com/authors/riley-edwards
amazon.com/author/rileyedwards

Printed in Great Britain
by Amazon